"I don't know

baby, Jack."

Rebecca's eyes flashed blue fire. "Even if you truly think I'm his mother," she continued, "instead of some other woman you encountered on your travels."

"You can't palm this off on another woman, Rebecca, so don't even try," Jack warned.

"Fine, I won't try to explain anything," she said furiously. "But in return, I want something from you, too, Jack Rourke."

Jack had the sinking feeling her request was going to be impossible to fulfil. "What?" he bit out, emotionally bracing himself for the worst.

Rebecca stomped nearer. "I want you to take your adorable little baby and leave this farm, me and Blair County forever," she fumed. "So I can forget my reckless affair with you ever happened!"

Dear Reader:

Romance readers have been enthusiastic about the Silhouette Special Editions for years. And that's not by accident: Special Editions were the first of their kind and continue to feature realistic stories with heightened romantic tension.

The longer stories, sophisticated style, greater sensual detail and variety that made Special Editions popular are the same elements that will make you want to read book after book.

We hope that you enjoy this Special Edition today, and will enjoy many more.

Please write to us:

Jane Nicholls
Silhouette Books
PO Box 236
Thornton Road
Croydon
Surrey
CR9 3RU

Daddy to the Rescue

CATHY GILLEN THACKER

All the characters in this book have no existence outside the imagination of the author, and have no relation whatsoever to anyone bearing the same name or names. They are not even distantly inspired by any individual known or unknown to the author, and all the incidents are pure invention.

First published in Great Britain 1996
by Silhouette Books, Eton House, 18-24 Paradise Road,
Richmond, Surrey TW9 1SR

ISBN 0 373 16526 9

23-9607

Made and printed in Great Britain

Chapter One

Pennsylvania Turnpike
April, 1993

"Are you trying to get yourself killed?" Jack Rourke jumped from his car and strode toward the beautiful young woman pacing the narrow sidewalk next to the curving tile wall. "You can't park your car in the middle of a tunnel!"

"I did not *park* my car!" the slender blonde in Amish clothing shouted back. Her posture was defiant as she struggled to be heard above the roar of the cars that were zooming by, one after another, in the unobstructed left lane. "It just *stopped,* and now it won't start!"

A truck approached directly behind their cars, switched lanes at the very last second and then zoomed by at teeth-rattling speed. "Look, we've got to get your car out of here before there's an accident." Jack directed the young woman toward the passenger side of her car. He jerked open the rusty door. "Get in, and put your car in neutral."

"But—"

"I'm going to push your car out of here with mine. As soon as you're out of the tunnel, steer the car over onto the shoulder and park it. We'll deal with the malfunctioning engine when we can do so safely."

Her face white, she slid across the seat to the driver's side. Jack got behind the wheel of his rental car. As soon as she put her car in neutral, it began to slide backward, down the incline. He inched his car forward. There was a jolt as the bumper on his car connected with hers. Jack gunned his engine, hoping that the Ford Mustang he'd rented had enough power to push her aging Chevy Caprice uphill.

In his rearview mirror, he could see two cars coming up on them, going side by side in the two-mile-long tunnel. They were travelling fast. At the last minute, the car directly behind Jack saw his flashing emergency lights, braked with a squeal and cut in behind the other car and in front of yet another eighteen-wheel truck. Sweat on his brow, Jack Rourke pushed the Mustang accelerator all the way to the floor. For one long frustrating second, he thought he was not going to be able to push the Amish woman's car out of the way, but finally the Chevy began to move forward.

As soon as they were out of the tunnel, both cars were pelted with rain. Above, the lightning flashed and the night sky rumbled with thunder. She steered her car onto the shoulder and hit the brake. Jack tucked his car in behind hers. He left his flashing lights on, as did she, then circled around to the passenger side of her car and opened the door. "My name's Jack

Rourke, by the way." He motioned her out. "Come on. I'll take you to a phone."

"Thank you, Mr. Rourke, but you've assisted me quite enough for one evening. You may be on your way now."

Right, Jack thought, like he could just leave her here, stranded on the side of a road. She couldn't have been more than twenty-three or twenty-four at most. And though she didn't look quite as innocent and sheltered as most of the Amish women he'd met the past few weeks, she was also not nearly as streetwise as she seemed to think she was. "You can't stay here."

"I can't leave my car."

Jack was getting drenched, standing there in the rain. Lightning flashed and thunder pounded like cannons in the black night sky overhead. "Look, Miss—"

"Lindholm." She sent him a challenging smile, as if she was just waiting for him to try to talk her into something she didn't want to do.

Jack had a feeling this woman was more than a match for him. "Is there a first name with that?" he drawled.

She kept her eyes on his. "Rebecca."

Damn, but she was distracting, Jack thought. He cleared his throat. "There should be a service center up the road, at the next turnpike exit. We can call for a tow truck from there."

Rebecca frowned. "I don't have money for a tow truck."

Jack shrugged. "Then I'll put it on my credit card and you can pay me back later. Or not. It really doesn't matter."

He had always wanted to rescue a beautiful damsel in distress. And she was very beautiful. He'd never seen such delicate bone structure or light blue eyes. Rebecca Lindholm was definitely of Scandinavian descent. Her skin was fair, flawless and looked as soft as silk to the touch. Her cheeks were a natural pink, as were her soft, incredibly kissable lips. And even though her hair was tucked up underneath a white organdy kapp, he could see enough of it to know it was a natural white blond. It, too, looked soft and silky to the touch. So soft and inviting, in fact, that he found himself wanting to take that kapp of hers off, her hair down, so he could sift his fingers through it and see how it looked resting on her slender shoulders . . .

Rebecca shook her head, cutting short his romantic imaginings. "You don't understand. I have to deliver these quilts to a store in Philadelphia first thing tomorrow morning."

Jack glanced behind him and for the first time noticed the stacks of quilts in the back. "Then I'll drive you the rest of the way to Philadelphia tonight, after we get your car to a service station. I'm heading to Philadelphia anyway to catch a flight back to Los Angeles tomorrow afternoon, so it's no trouble." Even if it had been out of his way, he would have taken her.

"Thank you, but I'll stay here and wait for another Amish family to come along and offer their assistance."

The chances of that happening were next to nil, Jack knew. Few Amish drove cars. Even fewer would be foolish enough to be out on the road on a night like tonight. And Rebecca Lindholm, for all her fragile blond beauty and feisty strength, was a walking target in her plain blue Amish dress, black apron, thick black stockings and thick black spinster shoes. But there was no reason to scare her with stories of other stranded motorists who'd come to unfortunate ends. Better to coax her into cooperating, Jack thought. "Why wait for someone who may or may not come along when you've already got me here, ready and willing to help you out?"

Rebecca looked at Jack a long moment. Evidently deciding that she could trust him enough to get into the car with him, she said slowly, "You're sure it would be no bother to drive me to Philadelphia?"

Jack did the best he could to hide his relief. "None at all. I'll even call for a tow truck."

"Oh, there's no need for that. I'll come back for my car tomorrow," she said.

So much for talking sense into Rebecca Lindholm, Jack thought, then decided to take it one moment at a time. They'd deal with tomorrow, tomorrow. The first order of business was transferring those quilts from her car to his.

She had no raincoat. Neither did Jack. Both were drenched to the skin by the time they had finished moving the quilts. "I'm surprised your family permits you to be out driving alone this time of night," Jack said as he guided his Mustang back onto the turnpike.

She shrugged carelessly. "My grandparents know I can take care of myself."

He took his eyes from the road to look at her. Her soft, bare lips were set in a stubborn line. "And they don't worry about you?"

"I'm a capable driver, before dark or after," she said.

He noticed she was shivering from the damp and the cold. He turned up the car heater and adjusted the vents to blow the majority of the warm air her way. He relaxed as she began to look more comfortable. "What about your husband?"

"I no longer have a husband."

Which meant she was probably a widow, Jack thought. The Amish didn't believe in divorce. "Your beloved then," he corrected.

Rebecca sent him a wry glance, as if secretly amused that he should be so curious about her love life. "I have no beloved, either. So. What are you doing in Pennsylvania if you don't live here?"

"I'm a screenwriter. I came back for a couple of weeks, to do some research for a movie on the Amish." Jack paused, wondering just how sheltered this woman was. "You do...know what movies are?"

"Yes," she said quietly, in a way that let him know she had taken offense. "I do."

"Sorry," Jack apologized reflexively as he tried not to notice how the sunny, springlike scent of her filled up his car and invaded his senses. "I didn't know how strict a sect you are from. I guess, since you're driving a car, you must be from one of the more progressive New Order sects." Jack knew from his research that the bishop for each community made rules that varied greatly from place to place. Obviously Rebecca Lindholm had more access to the outside or "English" world than most Amish women. In his view, that made her all the more fascinating. "Did you make all those quilts?" Jack inclined his head in the direction of the back seat.

"No. I'm the sales agent for all of the women in my community. Once a month, I take the quilts in to Philadelphia for sale."

Jack noted by the highway signs they were getting close to Philadelphia. Soon it would be time to drop her off. He wished his time with Rebecca Lindholm wasn't so limited. Then again, maybe it was just as well. He was leaving tomorrow. What was the point of starting something that had no future? "Do you have reservations at a hotel?" Jack asked.

Rebecca nodded her head and to his sharp disappointment—wasn't it his dumb fool luck to finally meet the woman of his dreams, only to have to promptly say goodbye?—she began to give him directions.

"I'M SORRY, Ms. Lindholm, but your reservations were canceled when you did not arrive by 4:00 p.m."

Rebecca sighed. This night was turning into an unmitigated disaster. She had thought she was doomed when her car quit midway up the tunnel through the mountain. Having Jack arrive to rescue her was like something out of a movie. But then, he said he wrote movies. Maybe he enjoyed acting like the forceful heroes he undoubtedly wrote about.

"Another room then—" Jack said.

"The Penn Relays are going on this week," the clerk explained with an efficient smile that said no matter how much he wanted to help them, there was nothing he could do to change the situation. "We're fully booked. Have been for months now."

"Want to try someplace else?" Jack turned to her, towering over her.

Rebecca looked up into his dark blue eyes and nodded. She normally didn't give much thought to a person's looks one way or another, but in Jack Rourke's case, she just couldn't help it. He was tremendously good-looking in a rough-hewn way that appealed to her on a very physical, very fundamental level. Unlike her own fair complexion, his skin was golden brown, hinting at year-round exposure to the sun. His jaw was ruggedly chiseled and clean-shaven, his lips masculine and firm. His eyes were direct and probing, and sincere.

He had a protective manner she liked, shoulders that were plenty wide enough for a woman to lean on and strong enough to do any of the hard physical labor required on a farm. His chest and stomach looked just as muscled. Lower still, she could see the firm outlines of his long, muscled legs beneath the fluid material of his much-washed jeans. As for the other, well . . . there was no way she was going to look there. She was much too tempted already. Which meant the sooner they found a hotel room for her, and they parted company, the better.

Unfortunately it wasn't that easy. Three hotels later, they were forced to confront the truth. With one of the world's largest track meets going on in Philadelphia, finding a hotel room after midnight was an impossible task.

She was about to suggest he drop her at a train station or the airport, and she would spend the night there, when he said in obvious exasperation, "Look, it's not getting any earlier. I'm staying at a friend's place. Alec Roman, you may have heard of him. Roman Computers..." He shook his head at her blank look. "Never mind. Anyway, you're welcome to come home with me. There's no one else there and the place is big enough. If you want to stay there, I'll get you wherever you need to be in the morning."

It was a matter-of-fact invitation, casually delivered. Yet her heart was pounding. Rebecca forced herself to draw a calming breath. "I couldn't possibly impose," she said, even though part of her wanted to.

"It's not an imposition," Jack said, smiling at her in a very inviting way.

Rebecca hesitated. "You say Mr. Roman would not mind?" She searched his eyes, looking for some selfish purpose there, but to her relief could find none.

"Alec's in Japan, and no, he wouldn't mind." Jack touched her shoulder gently and turned her in the direction of the lobby door. "Alec and I are old friends. That's why I'm staying there instead of in a hotel."

Rebecca allowed Jack to open the car door for her. Staying with Jack seemed safer than spending the night in the train station. "I'll stay there, then," she decided.

His relief that the matter had been settled evident, Jack drove to Alec Roman's mansion on Society Hill. They entered the open wrought-iron gates and drove up the circular driveway in silence.

Located in a picturesque area with cobblestone streets and plentiful parks, the three-story redbrick home boasted a mansard roof with dormer windows. Pine green shutters adorned every window. The front door was painted a glossy white. Smokestacks had been built at each end of the house. Tall hedges and an abundance of mature trees provided privacy while adding greatly to the elegant, pastoral setting.

As Jack parked the rental car in front of the brick mansion, Rebecca worked hard to keep her face expressionless, but inwardly she was reeling. This home was incredible... and unhappily, a lot like the home of her ex-husband's family. Memories of her tumultuous romantic past assaulted her.

Jack grabbed his own suitcase and Rebecca's satchel. Together, they headed up the walk. Inside, the ivy-covered century-old mansion was everything Jack would have expected it to be. A sweeping staircase dominated the marble-floored front hall. A chandelier sparkled overhead. To the right was a banquet-size dining room. To the left, a formal living room filled with antiques. To the rear of that, a paneled study with a huge fireplace and a gourmet kitchen with every electric appliance imaginable.

They walked back to the front hall, after the brief tour. Rebecca knew what was next. A tour of the second floor, where the bedrooms were. That, she suddenly did not want to do. "The quilts—" Rebecca said, her heart suddenly pounding again.

"They'll be fine in the car," Jack reassured her bluntly.

Rebecca shook her head in disagreement. "They were dampened with the rain. I need to dry them."

Jack strode to the front door and looked at the rain, which was still coming down in buckets.

"Perhaps if you pulled the car into the garage," Rebecca said.

"Can't. It has a separate security code, and Alec forgot to leave it to me. If I try to open it from the inside, the alarms will go off. It's not a problem. I'll carry them in."

"I'll help." Once they'd brought everything in, Jack helped her spread the quilts out to air-dry. When they'd finished, he turned to face her, his expression bemused. "Hey," he teased, touching a finger to the tip of her nose. "You're all wet."

Rebecca looked at the raindrops glistening on the strands of his thick chestnut hair. "So are you."

As he watched her shiver, his expression became concerned. "You'd better change into something warm and dry before you catch cold."

Rebecca frowned. "I've only got one other dress and apron with me, and I'll need those for tomorrow."

Jack nodded. "I understand that you want to look nice when you go to do business at the department store, but you can't stay in wet clothes."

Nor could she change into her nightgown, and still be around him. And she wasn't quite ready to go to bed yet. She wanted to talk to Jack, find out more about him, and his life in Los Angeles. "My clothes will dry eventually," she insisted.

"Faster," Jack pointed out, "if they're in the dryer."

Unable to help herself, Rebecca shivered again. Jack went to the thermostat and kicked it up from sixty to seventy-two. "This place takes a while to heat up." He frowned as she turned even paler. "Much more of this chill air in those damp clothes and your lips will be turning blue. I'll get you some clothes to change into. And something hot to drink."

REBECCA'S FINGERS trembled as she removed her black apron and then her long blue dress. Her underclothes were similarly drenched. Hesitating only a moment, she removed everything including her long black socks, then stood cradling the men's clothing Jack had given her. What would her family think if they could see her now? she wondered, then decided it was too cold to dawdle. She slipped on the soft gray cotton sweatshirt and pants. They were baggy and too long on her, but very warm and thick. Next came the thick white men's socks—also too big—and then a thick navy blue robe made of terry cloth. She belted it around her awkwardly, then picked up her wet clothing.

She hadn't worn English clothing since she'd been married. She had forgotten how comfortable it could be. Just as she'd forgotten what it was like to want to be kissed and held by a man. But that wasn't going to happen tonight, she told herself firmly. She might be attracted to Jack Rourke, but they were worlds apart. She couldn't let herself forget that. Her emotions tightly in check, she picked up her bundle of wet clothes and headed downstairs.

Jack was in the laundry room off the kitchen, tossing damp clothes into the electric washing machine. He had changed into a dark blue corduroy shirt and blue jeans. He was wearing thick white socks, like the ones he had given her, and a pair of running shoes. "There you are," he said with a smile. "I was beginning to wonder if maybe you'd fallen asleep up there."

Rebecca shook her head. "Though I probably should be in bed, considering the late hour."

"It's been a stressful evening. We probably both need to unwind." He took the clothes from her and tossed them into the machine. "We ought to be able to wash them all together on cold," he said. "Except for these." He brought out a handful of hand-sewn white linen underthings. "These had probably better be washed out by hand or on the delicate cycle."

Rebecca flushed to her roots, despite herself. "I agree."

"Perhaps you'd like to take care of them?" he said gently.

She nodded self-consciously. Jack showed her where everything was, then left the room. "I'll be in the kitchen, making us something to eat," he said over his shoulder.

Rebecca quickly rinsed out her underthings in the laundry-room sink and put them into the dryer to dry. It took a moment, but she figured out how to use the dials and switched it on, then joined him in the kitchen. He was completely at ease at the stove. A tray was set up on the counter beside him. Seeing the thick sandwiches and tall glasses of milk, Rebecca was reminded of how long it had been since she'd eaten.

"Let's go in the study, by the fire," Jack said when he'd finished pouring steaming soup into two mugs. "It's warmer there."

The study was a large room, filled with books, and a desk and a computer. There was a coffee table in front of a large leather sofa. Jack set the tray down and sat on one end of the sofa. Rebecca sat on the other. "Do you always travel at night?" Jack asked, handing her a sandwich on a plate and a mug of soup.

Rebecca balanced her plate and mug on her lap and wondered if this whole evening felt as much like something out of a movie to him as it did to her. She frowned as she lifted the mug of soup to her lips. "No. I should have left earlier."

"Why didn't you?" Jack asked, his dark blue eyes taking on a concerned gleam.

"I wanted to see my friend's new baby." Rebecca paused and took a sip of the hot, delicious soup. "I didn't mean to stay that long. But she was so cute and sweet . . ."

"And you adore babies."

"And I adore babies, and I got to talking." Rebecca sighed her lament. "I always lose track of the time when I'm around babies and I get to talking."

Jack grinned at her as if he understood perfectly. "So when were you supposed to arrive in Philadelphia?"

"Long before dark." She couldn't begin to describe the panic she had felt when her car had broken down in the middle of that tunnel. All those trucks thundering past, the storm raging outside... And then her hero came charging in to save her. The more she looked at Jack, the more she realized he was a hero—a flesh-and-blood, real-life hero, even though he might not realize it.

"Will anyone be worried about you?" Jack asked gently.

"No."

"Your grandparents—"

"Will think I am at the hotel where I am supposed to be."

"Do you want to call them?"

Rebecca turned to him, unable to help but notice the way the soft light of the study gilded the rugged lines of his face. "They don't have a telephone, nor do any of my neighbors. I'll just explain what happened . . ." *Most* of what happened, Rebecca amended silently, "when I get home again."

Jack nodded. "And home is where?"

"A farm in Blair County."

Jack finished his sandwich. He leaned back, looking remarkably content. "Well, I'm glad we met," he said as he put his plate aside and picked up his mug.

"Why?"

He sipped his soup and regarded her warmly over the rim of his mug. "Because you're the type of person I'd like to count among my friends."

Unnerved by his assumption there could be something more between them than tonight, Rebecca stood and moved restlessly to the fire. She had taken her kapp off upstairs, because it didn't seem to go with the sweats, but left her hair in a braid. Unfortunately her hair was still damp and it was beginning to bother her. Without looking at Jack, she began to undo the braid. "We have nothing in common, Jack."

"Maybe more than you give us credit for," he said as he closed the distance between them languorously and lounged against the mantel.

Rebecca looked away from the disturbing heat in his eyes. She combed her fingers through her hair, aware she was suddenly breathing so fast she felt a little dizzy. And hot. "Such as?"

"You're naturally curious, just like I am. I saw it in your eyes when we walked in, the way you looked around. And you're headstrong, independent to a fault. You'd have to be to be out driving alone on a night like tonight."

Rebecca gazed into the fire and tried to ignore the tantalizing way her insides warmed at his nearness. Or the way she tingled with anticipation. He smelled so good. Like a pine tree, surrounded by freshly fallen snow. Being with Jack was like being in a warm wonderful dream that had little to do with the harsher realities of life.

"And you're an artist," Jack continued, withdrawing a small comb from his back pocket and handing it to her wordlessly. "You'd have to be to design one of those quilts."

Rebecca tugged the comb through the thick, damp waves of her hair. Jack watched, his eyes dark with desire.

She was aware she was playing with fire here, but she couldn't seem to stop herself. She had been alone for so long now, and she knew, given the way she felt about all the eligible Amish men she knew, she was likely to stay unmarried, too. Without warning, Jack stalked away from her. He crossed to the desk and stood riffling through a stack of papers.

"Listen, anytime you want to go up is fine with me. I'll stay down here and put the clothes in the dryer."

Rebecca hated the look in his eyes right now. So distant, and aloof, as if he wanted to be anywhere but here with her. And though she knew he was wise to pull back before anything happened between them, a part of her, a deeply feminine part, resented his ability to walk away from her when she couldn't seem to walk away from him at all.

She put the comb down and crossed to his side. "Don't, Rebecca," Jack replied tersely, but wouldn't look her in the eye.

"Don't what?" she whispered.

He lifted his head and turned to face her. "You shouldn't push this," he said, his eyes hard, warning her away. "Because I can't guarantee what'll happen if you do."

"You think I'm so innocent—" she murmured as he tilted her face up to his, so she had no choice but to look into his dark blue eyes. And he was so wrong. She'd been married, loved... She knew what was happening here. And she was feeling reckless enough to want it to happen.

"Dammit, Rebecca, you *are* innocent, at least by my world's standards," Jack insisted on a ragged breath as he laced his other hand protectively around her waist, holding her apart from him.

"No—"

"I'll show you," he said, pulling her close, as if he meant to teach her a lesson, to show her more of the world than he thought she already knew.

Rebecca was braced to resist his high-handedness, but as his mouth touched hers, everything changed. A jolt of passion surged through her like an electric current. It was followed swiftly by incredible longing, the kind she had only dreamed about, and a wealth of erotic sensations. In an instant, Rebecca felt she knew what it was to be loved and wanted, and she struggled to give back as much as she was receiving, opening her mouth to his strong, demanding kisses, twining her tongue with his.

The sudden flare of passion in Rebecca, the way she trembled in his arms and surged against him, confirmed Jack's masculine instincts. He could hardly believe it, but it was true; she wanted him as much as he wanted her. And that knowledge, as well as his own burgeoning ardor, swamped his senses. He had always felt that somewhere there was a woman for him, a woman who would captivate and enthrall and drive him mad with desire. At last, he thought, he had found her.

"Rebecca—" he murmured, reaching for the belt on the borrowed robe she wore. His robe. He released it, slid his hand inside, beneath the hem of the sweatshirt and up over her waist, her ribs, to the softness of one very round, very full breast. She gasped as he palmed the soft curves and caressed her nipple. It budded tightly in response as she shivered and sagged heavily against him. "I want you, Rebecca."

"I know," she whispered, drawing back to look up at him. Her light blue eyes were filled with wonder and longing. "I want you, too."

Her soft words were all the encouragement he needed. Jack swung Rebecca up into his arms and headed for the stairs to the bedroom where he'd been staying. Inside was a big four-poster bed. He hadn't really appreciated the romance of it, until now. Rebecca made no protest as he laid her gently down on the center of it. "Still time to change your mind," he said as he covered her body with the warmth of his. Whatever happened next, he wanted her to be sure.

But Rebecca didn't want to change her mind, any more than she wanted him to leave. She laced her arms around his neck and with the pressure of her fingertips against his nape, brought his head back down to hers. He covered her mouth in a deep, lingering kiss. He was rewarded with an arch of her body, and a low, soft moan that streamed across his senses like soft, warm rain. His lower body throbbing with anticipation, he nudged her legs apart and slid between them. Tucking a hand inside the waistband of her sweats, he found the softest part of her and sought to discover every velvet curve.

As he stroked her intimately, she began to writhe. He eased his fingers into her damp heat, and felt her arch again. Over and over he stroked, until she clung to him almost mindlessly, whispering his name, clutching his shoulders, and suddenly, he couldn't hold back, either. His lower body swollen, hot and aching, he struggled out of his clothes and helped her out of hers. The next thing he knew she was urging him into her, holding him tightly sheathed inside. Almost beside himself with pleasure, Jack groaned and slipped his hands beneath her. His whole body throbbing and demanding satiation, he lifted her up into his thrusts. Their mouths mated as intimately as their bodies, and long moments later, when their climax came, they were still kissing as deeply and intimately as ever. Only when their bodies relaxed, when their trembling and shuddering had ceased, did they slowly, languorously move apart.

"Rebecca—" He hesitated, not sure he could find the right words to explain the depth and intensity of his feelings for her, not sure she would believe him if he did. And yet he wanted so much to say them.

"I know, Jack," she whispered, reaching for him once again. "I know..."

JACK WOKE TO FIND the first rays of daylight streaming in through the open draperies. After their wild night of truly incredible, absolutely unforgettable lovemaking, he had expected to find Rebecca still in his bed, curled up against him. Instead, she was gone. He thought about going after her, then decided against it. She obviously wanted it to be over. And although that wasn't what he wanted, he would do the chivalrous thing and respect her wishes.

Chapter Two

11 months later
Blair County, Pennsylvania

Jack Rourke glanced down at the adorable infant in the car seat beside him and wondered for the millionth time how Rebecca Lindholm could have deserted their baby. So maybe she hadn't wanted a child born as the result of their admittedly reckless one-night stand nearly a year ago, but did that mean she had to put the two-month-old Andy in a heart-shaped red wicker basket decorated with stenciled cupids and a white satin bow, and then just leave him on Alec Roman's doorstep on Valentine's Day?

And what about that note she'd left with Andy—*"To Andy's father... Own up to your mistakes!"* Could she really consider Andy, with his cherubic angel's face, long-lashed big blue eyes and dark curly hair, a mistake? Jack sure didn't. *He* had fallen in love with Andy the instant he'd flown in from Los Angeles and laid eyes on him. And the two of them had been happily bonding in the forty-eight hours since.

So how was it that Rebecca, who'd evidently had custody of baby Andy for the first two months or so of his life, had been able to just abandon their baby on a doorstep? Had she felt so overwhelmed by the responsibility that she'd had no choice but to take Andy to the place where she and Jack had spent that one magical night together and just leave him and hope for the best?

Granted, because of the clandestine way she had walked out on him that night last spring, Rebecca had had no other way to contact Jack except through Alec. But ringing the doorbell and leaving Andy on the doorstep still seemed a little heartless, no matter how desperate for help Rebecca had been.

But then again, Jack thought, it fit. Rebecca had run from Jack once. Maybe she had just been running from Andy, too. Maybe that was how she coped with stressful situations.

"I guess we'll find out what your mom was thinking soon enough, though, won't we, sport?" Jack told Andy as he turned his rental car off the Pennsylvania turnpike and into the restaurant parking lot. "Because like it or not, your mom's time for running is over. We're going to deal with this situation the way we should have from the very first, as a family."

At the sound of Jack's determined voice, Andy kicked and gurgled in response.

Deciding his son probably needed a diaper change after the long drive to Blair County, Jack unbuckled his seat belt and reached for the diaper bag. Leaving the car engine running and the heater on, he unstrapped Andy and lifted him out of his combination carrier/car seat. Pushing that aside, he laid Andy gently on the seat beside him. Quickly he unzipped Andy's white cashmere bunting outfit, and lifted him out of it.

The back door opened just as Jack laid Andy gently back on the seat.

"Are you trying to ruin me?" Rebecca Lindholm demanded in a high, agitated voice as she slid into the back seat of the sedan and shut the door. Jack understood her concern. From where they were sitting, they could be seen by anyone coming and going in the late February afternoon. Fortunately the combination gas station, restaurant and gift shop was crowded with more travelers just passing through than locals interested in gossip.

"No, of course I'm not," Jack said, hardly able to believe he and Rebecca were together again. So many times he'd thought he'd dreamed, or perhaps just enhanced his recollection, of the electricity between them. But he saw now it wasn't true. Even with her Nordic blond hair tucked neatly beneath her white organdy kapp, her fair cheeks pink with embarrassment, Rebecca was every bit as angelically beautiful as he recalled.

Merely looking at her made his pulse quicken and his lower half tighten with desire. Just as merely thinking about what she'd done made his heart twist with pain. He met her temperamental glance and struggled to hold on to his own soaring emotions. He knew he hadn't exactly played fair, tracking her down through her work just to see her again, but she hadn't given him much choice.

"Then what do you call getting my address from the Philadelphia department store where I market quilts?" Rebecca demanded.

"The act of a desperate man. Not to worry, Rebecca. I told them I wanted to commission a quilt. Nothing more."

She sucked in a quick, agitated breath. "And is that what you really want from me, Jack?"

"No, of course not," Jack replied harshly.

"Then what?"

"I want you to own up to your responsibilities," he corrected quietly.

"What responsibilities?"

"To Andy here!"

Rebecca spared baby Andy a brief puzzled glance. Andy gurgled and cooed at Rebecca with unabashed delight, which just proved to Jack that Andy remembered his mother...if not the way she had abandoned him.

"Whose child is this, Jack?" Rebecca asked.

As if she didn't know! Jack thought. "Mine," he said roughly. *And yours.*

"Oh." Rebecca stared at Andy again, this time...in shock?

Mindful that Andy was beginning to get a little restless, Jack unsnapped Andy's light blue sleeper with the embroidered bunnies on the front, removed the soggy diaper and replaced it with a fresh disposable diaper.

He started to fasten the adhesive tape on the side. "You forgot the baby powder," Rebecca pointed out in a low, dull tone.

Jack lifted a brow at Rebecca. He found it ironic she was giving him advice on how to properly care for their son after the way she had behaved. "Thanks for the reminder," he said gruffly, "and the baby has a name."

Rebecca stiffened. "I'm sure he does. However, as I've never seen him before in my life, I wouldn't know it."

"Yeah, right," Jack agreed dryly. How much more of this innocent act did Rebecca really expect him to buy? He reached for the powder, and while Andy continued to coo and kick, he sprinkled his bottom, then finished the diapering task. "The next thing you know you'll be telling me you've never seen me before, either."

Rebecca flushed as she watched Jack refasten Andy's sleeper and rezip his bunting outfit. Evidently satisfied he had done the job properly, she returned her fiery gaze to his face. "I wasn't aware you had a baby, Jack."

"Neither was I until two days ago."

Rebecca's shock deepened, then recognition dawned on her face. "Is that why you've come to see me? Because you need a nanny for your son and you remembered how much I love babies?"

"Actually, Rebecca, I had in mind a lot more than that."

"I have no interest in working for you or your wife, Jack."

"I'm not married."

Rebecca leaned forward. "Then where is this child's mother?"

"I was hoping you could tell me that," Jack retorted dryly.

"How would I know where this child's mother is?" Rebecca asked, incensed.

Jack glared at her. "You're really determined to play this game until the bitter end, aren't you?"

"What game?" Rebecca hissed right back. "You're the one who is playing games with me. Why, I don't know. Unless..." Rebecca paused. "You're angry because of the way I left you that night last spring."

Now they were getting somewhere, Jack thought. "Wouldn't you be?"

"Okay, so maybe I shouldn't have left the way I did, but... the way things were... it seemed like the best thing to do."

The best thing? For whom? Jack wondered, recalling his consternation when he'd woken up alone.

Jack put on Andy's hat, then grabbed a bottle from the diaper bag. "You couldn't have stayed around long enough to get my address and phone number? Because you know if you had, you would've been able to contact me personally, instead of dumping this in Alec Roman's lap. And I'm going to need to go into the restaurant to get this bottle warmed for Andy." Jack got out of the car, a squirming Andy in his arms, Rebecca fast on his heels.

"I don't know what you're talking about," she whispered as she glanced furtively around them to make sure no one was watching or listening to their conversation. "I never met Alec Roman."

Jack strode nonchalantly toward the front door of the diner. "Only because you ran before Alec could answer the doorbell," he remarked.

Because Jack's arms were full, Rebecca held the door for him and Andy, then fell into step after Jack as he walked toward a booth in the back.

Loud enough for the others in the diner to hear, she said to Jack, "I think it would be possible to commission a series of quilts, but we should talk first, to determine what colors you would prefer, Mr. Rourke."

"That would be fine, Miss Lindholm," Jack said, just as loudly, then sat down, Andy in his arms. Rebecca sat opposite him. The waitress brought them menus and she left with Andy's bottle, promising to warm it carefully.

Alone with Jack again, Rebecca removed her bonnet and her cloak. She smiled at him superficially. "Let's start at the beginning. Why do you think I should know this baby? And what responsibilities are you talking about? I have no responsibilities to you!"

Jack had to hand it to her, she was quite an actress. His mouth tightened in a mixture of contempt and disapproval. "What about your responsibilities to Andy?"

Rebecca leaned across the table toward him. The pink color highlighting her high, delicate cheekbones grew even pinker. "I have none to him, either. Furthermore, I resent your coming here to see me this way.''

''Well that's just too bad, Rebecca,'' Jack murmured back, keeping his voice deceptively casual to keep from alarming Andy, who was already squirming anxiously, awaiting his bottle. ''Because I'm not going away, and neither is Andy, until we've settled things between us. And while we're on the subject, I resent the way you've been behaving, too.''

''You cannot continue talking to me like this in a public place,'' Rebecca whispered, casting a furtive glance around them. To her relief, no one in the crowded restaurant was paying the least attention to them. She was just another Amish woman in a state crowded with Amish, talking to an English man. ''It might get back to my family.''

Jack glanced pointedly down at Andy—who was sitting so happily in his baby carrier—then back at her. How any woman could turn away from such a darling baby, he didn't know. But it hurt him to think that she had. ''Like the fact you had my baby won't,'' he pointed out wryly.

''What are you talking about?'' Rebecca's hand flew to the bodice of her starched blue cotton dress. ''I haven't had a baby!'' Jack merely quirked a brow. Her blue eyes narrowed suspiciously. ''Where did you really get this child, Jack?''

''As if you don't know,'' Jack retorted sarcastically.

Her cheeks went from pink to scarlet. She drew her black wool cloak closer and cast another furtive look around her. "Listen to me, Jack. I do not want to play games with you."

"Fine. Then stop the innocent act and start dealing with the plain and simple facts of the matter."

"I will, just as soon as you start explaining what you think—erroneously, I might add—is going on here."

Because Andy's dark brow furrowed with every increasingly emotional syllable he and Rebecca spoke, Jack took a deep breath and attempted a softer, more conciliatory tack. "Look, Rebecca, I can understand why you'd want to keep Andy's birth a secret. Your community would shun you if they knew. But ignoring our child is not going to make him or me go away."

Rebecca rolled her eyes. "Oh, I can see that."

"There were better ways to deal with this, Rebecca," Jack continued softly but firmly. He leaned toward her earnestly. "You should have tracked me down as soon as you discovered you were pregnant," he said as Andy gurgled happily beside them and waved his hands in front of his face. "I would have come back and done the honorable thing."

Rebecca smiled at Andy, then turned back to Jack and glared at him as if he were nuts. The waitress appeared with Andy's bottle. She stayed only long enough to take their order—coffee and pie for both of them—before disappearing again.

Jack uncapped the bottle and tested it on his wrist. The formula was lukewarm. Perfect.

Rebecca watched as Jack picked Andy up out of his baby carrier and settled him comfortably in the crook of his arm. Sure Andy was settled comfortably, Jack turned his glance back to Rebecca. "If you'd rather do this—" he offered. "After all, as his mother, you have every right."

Abruptly, Rebecca looked like she was about to explode. She leaned toward him and hissed, very, very quietly, "For the last time, Jack, Andy is not my baby. Furthermore, I don't know why you would think that he is."

"Oh, I don't know," he drawled. "Maybe the fact that Andy was left on Alec Roman's doorstep, which coincidentally happens to be the only place you know to contact me. Maybe the fact that we had one night of incredibly wild, wonderful sex approximately eleven months ago, and this baby is approximately two months old. And maybe the fact he has curly dark hair, like my mother's, and your incredible blue eyes."

Rebecca released a short, exasperated breath. "All fair-skinned babies are born with blue eyes, Jack! They don't necessarily stay blue. By the time the babies are six months old their eyes can be brown, or green, or gray."

"Nice try, Rebecca," Jack said dryly.

"It's true! The fact he was born with blue eyes means absolutely nothing!"

"Okay, maybe it doesn't," Jack allowed. "But all babies don't have your chin. Come on, Rebecca." He leaned toward her urgently. "Own up to your mistake, just as I've now owned up to mine." Jack noticed half of Andy's bottle was gone. It was time for a burp. "I can forgive you."

Rebecca's face flooded with color as Jack lifted Andy to his shoulder. "For the last time, Jack, Andy is not my baby. Now leave me alone." Giving him no chance to respond, she slid out of the booth, turned on her heel and marched defiantly out of the restaurant.

THE DOOR to the restaurant shut quietly behind her, but inside Rebecca was quaking. She couldn't believe Jack had come back into her life now, after all this time. Initially, yes, she had wanted to see him again, even though she knew their love was impossible. But he hadn't come to see her, and gradually she had given up hope of their ever meeting again. Only to have him show up now—with a baby, for heaven's sake!

If her grandparents heard about any of this . . . they would be so hurt. And if Jack didn't keep a lower profile, they might also be publicly embarrassed, and she couldn't let that happen. Not again. Her grandparents had already been through the pain of watching her marry one fickle Englishman. She couldn't put them through the same thing again, not when she knew how poorly mixed marriages fared in the real world.

Jack had romanticized her, and while that was flattering, it was also dangerous. She was not the pure angel he had first envisioned her, any more than she was the heartless baby-deserting mother he was accusing her of being now. She was human. And, as her unprecedented fling with him attested, all too impulsively romantic for her own good. She had to be sensible now, and that meant, sadly, walking away from him and this crazy notion he had gotten into his head. Andy might be Jack's baby—with another woman—but he was definitely not Rebecca's baby! Jack was going to have to understand that. Hopefully he already did.

In the meantime, she had quilts to collect for her monthly trip in to Philadelphia at the end of the week. The fickle February weather permitting, it would be another banner month for the women in her community, and the profits from the quilts would pay for their spring seed.

"REBECCA, come in and meet our visitor."

Rebecca stood in the doorway of her family's home, unable to believe what she was seeing. Her feet felt as if they had turned to stone.

"This is Jack Rourke, and his son, Andy. He is visiting the area to learn more about the Amish."

Rebecca looked at Jack. He was sitting in a straight-backed chair, a sleeping Andy curled contentedly against his broad chest. He couldn't have looked like a more loving, devoted father to his infant son had he tried. And worse, he had obviously swiftly won over her grandparents, too.

Seeing Jack so cozily ensconced in the light blue and white parlor made Rebecca want to faint and scream simultaneously. And darn him, he knew it, too. If Jack wanted a scene, however, he was going to be disappointed, Rebecca thought. She was just as determined to keep her grandparents out of this mess as Jack was determined to bring them into it.

Carefully Rebecca placed the two colorful quilts she had just collected for the month's sale on the shelf, and then removed her cloak and hung it up in the closet next to the door. Her emotions under control, she turned back to Jack with a reserved nod. "Good afternoon, Mr. Rourke." I should have known you wouldn't give up so easily, she thought resentfully.

Jack looked at her pointedly, in a frank easy way that made her heart race. "You know, I did some research here last summer. Perhaps we met—?"

"I do not recall your coming to our farm," Rebecca said, wishing she didn't recall with such utter clarity what it had been like to be held in those strong arms of his.

"No, I guess I didn't," Jack conceded reluctantly, his dark blue eyes never leaving hers. "Although I probably should have. Perhaps if I had met with your family then," he continued with a forthright smile, "I wouldn't have so many questions now."

Rebecca didn't know what game Jack was playing with her, but she did know two could play at it. "I'm not sure what we could tell you that would be of interest," Rebecca murmured as she breezed past him, to the kitchen at the other end of the open first floor.

"Oh, you'd be surprised," Jack retorted.

"Mr. Rourke is looking for a place to stay while he is in Blair County," Ruth said. Rebecca shot her grandmother an uneasy glance. Ruth was a very loving woman. But unlike Rebecca, she had been protected all her life from the outside world, and hence tended to be too naive for her own welfare.

"And we've agreed to let him stay with us," her grandfather, Eli, said.

"It's important the information I get be one-hundred percent correct," Jack said. "I want to make sure everything I've written to date, as well as any rewrites I may do in the next few weeks, are as accurate and truthful as I can make them."

Rebecca turned to her grandfather numbly.

"I am sure we can show him everything he needs to know about being Amish," her grandfather said.

"How long are you planning to be here, Mr. Rourke?" Rebecca asked. Her heart pounding, she walked to the cupboard, picked up a glass and poured herself some of the lemonade her grandmother had made.

"As long as it takes for me to find out what I need to know," Jack said, his dark blue eyes narrowing as he watched her gulp the drink swiftly, then put her glass into the sink. "And in exchange for your grandparents' hospitality, I have agreed to help with any and all chores assigned to me," Jack said.

Her grandmother glanced tenderly at the sleeping baby in Jack's arms. "Isn't he sweet?" Ruth said softly, reminding Rebecca how much her grandmother wanted great-grandchildren of her own.

Rebecca nodded, her thoughts in complete disarray. This was like a bad dream that would just not end. She swallowed and affected a normal tone. "I'll start dinner."

Jack rose after her, his expression implacable as he bent and gently settled a still-sleeping Andy into the hand-carved wooden cradle the Lindholms had provided him. "I'll help."

"MEN DON'T COOK in an Amish household."

Jack looked at Rebecca. He wasn't surprised by her home. The prosperous farm boasted several white barns, two silos and a neatly tended white frame house that looked at least half a century old. Her grandparents were warm, loving people. New Order Amish, they didn't seem the type to throw Rebecca out on her ear if she had revealed to them she was pregnant. But then, he thought, maybe appearances were deceptive in this case. Or maybe she just hadn't wanted to disappoint them. Maybe she hadn't come to terms with the fact she'd had a fling. Whatever the reason for Rebecca's strange behavior, he was determined to get to the bottom of it.

Aware she was still waiting for him to voice a reason why he should be permitted in her kitchen, Jack shrugged and said, "Well, I'm not Amish, and I do cook."

"I would appreciate your not helping me," Rebecca hissed. She glared at him in stubborn silence.

Jack regarded her calmly, letting her know with one look that if it was a waiting game she wanted to play, he would win.

"Is there a problem in here, Rebecca?" Eli's voice boomed from the other end of the room.

Her cheeks pink, her slender shoulders stiff with tension, Rebecca slowly turned to face her grandfather. "I don't wish to have Mr. Rourke help me in my kitchen," she stated plainly.

"How else will I learn the ins and outs of Amish cooking?" Jack asked casually, as he gently rocked Andy's cradle.

"My grandmother can show you, just as soon as she gets back from the root cellar," Rebecca said, giving both Jack and their son a wide berth as she stepped closer to the refrigerator that was, as far as Jack could see, one of the few modern conveniences Rebecca's family allowed themselves.

Eli cleared his throat and stepped closer, stroking his bearded jaw with one hand. Like Rebecca and his wife, Ruth, he was dressed starkly in plain black trousers and a simple blue shirt. "Perhaps it would be best if you started your chores here with something simpler," he said. "Have you ever gathered eggs?"

Jack grinned. "Can't say that I have."

To Jack's surprise, Eli looked at Rebecca. "Perhaps you can show him where the henhouse is, then, and help him get started before you come back in to begin cooking dinner with your grandmother."

"YOU'RE ANGRY with me for showing up here," Jack noted as the two of them stepped outside into the cold winter air. The sky above was a glum gray. Patches of half-melted snow dotted the ground here and there in a dismal-looking reminder of the last snowfall. Yet, despite the gloomy weather and his cool reception from Rebecca, Jack could never recall feeling more alive. Or enthused about the future. Maybe if Rebecca saw how determined he was to have her in his life again, she would open up to him.

"Don't pretend to be surprised about that!" Rebecca stormed angrily as she rushed past him, her black cloak flapping open in the wind. "I can't believe you actually talked my grandparents into letting you and your baby stay at our farm. Have you no conscience at all?"

"My conscience, Rebecca, is what brought me back here. I want our baby to have two parents. I would think you would want that, too," Jack said.

"He is not our baby, Jack, and no amount of wishing will ever make that so."

Jack noticed how the blue of Rebecca's dress brought out the blue of her eyes. The plain black apron, black stockings and schoolmarm shoes shouldn't have made her look sexy as hell, but they did. And that was making it hard for him to concentrate. "You're denying you left Andy in a basket on Alec Roman's doorstep on Valentine's Day?"

Rebecca's cheeks flooded with a healthy color that was, Jack felt, only partially due to the brisk winter wind. "Yes, Jack, I am," she said firmly.

He studied her upturned face. She was either a very good liar, or she was telling the truth...sort of. "Then who put Andy there for you, Rebecca?" Jack asked coolly.

Rebecca shook her head and rolled her eyes. "You are impossible!" she whispered emotionally.

Holding her voluminous skirts in both hands, Rebecca whirled and marched across the yard, through a fence and into a barnyard that was amazingly still and devoid of life. Jack followed at a leisurely pace, enjoying the view. More so, perhaps, because he knew beneath that prim dress beat the heart of a very passionate woman, a woman who had just given birth to his child, and who obviously now—despite all her protestations—wanted him and Andy back in her life. Otherwise, why would she have left Andy with Alec? Why not just raise Andy on her own?

Rebecca threw open the doors of the henhouse. Chickens squawked and flew every which way. While Jack watched, she scurried them along outside with swooping motions of her hands. Most of them went gratefully, anxious to be out in the yard. She followed the chickens back out, announcing, "We'll feed them now, too."

She took the lid from a can in the corner of the chicken yard, scattered scoops of grain liberally around the yard and watched in mute satisfaction as the chickens fell on it. She headed back inside the henhouse, leaving Jack to follow.

"The eggs are in the nests," Rebecca explained, making no effort to mask her impatience both with Jack and the task assigned her by her grandfather. She picked up an egg and put it in a wicker basket. "Gather them all, put the chickens back in the henhouse, close it up and then bring the eggs back inside the house. We'll wash them in the kitchen." She turned, offering him her back.

"Wait a minute," Jack said, grabbing her arm, beginning to panic. He was a city kid, always had been, always would be. What did he know about rounding up chickens? He tightened his hold on her. "You can't leave me here."

Rebecca disdainfully removed his fingers from her arm. "I have to start dinner."

He stepped to bar her way out of the barnyard, fully prepared to hold her in front of him with both hands if necessary. "Dinner can wait," he said, setting the baskets down for a moment. "What about Andy? Don't you think you have some explaining to do?"

She looked past him toward the house, her expression more aggrieved than ever. "I've already said everything there is to say."

"You can't possibly mean that," he said, aghast.

Rebecca looked down her pretty nose at him. The brisk winter wind brought even more color to her high, graceful cheeks. "I mean that with my whole heart and soul," she retorted.

Seeing the stubborn denial in her eyes, it was all he could do not to haul her into his arms and kiss her senseless. But he knew he had to try reason first. "We have a child, Rebecca," he said softly, determined to make her come to terms with the situation. "A beautiful child. I know you're afraid, but I can fix everything." After all, Eli seemed like a reasonable man. Ruth was certainly loving. They would want what was best for Rebecca, he was sure of it. And what was best for Rebecca was being with him and Andy.

"You can fix everything," Rebecca repeated sarcastically. She planted a hand on his chest and arched a coolly disarming brow. "Including your runaway imagination?"

Jack couldn't help it, he laughed. Then he caught her hand, and pulled her ever closer. Close enough so that she could feel the strong, steady beating of his heart beneath the corduroy shirt and open leather bomber jacket.

For a moment Rebecca's eyes widened with shock. Her lips parted with desire. Recovering swiftly, she jerked her hand away. "I don't know where you got that baby, Jack." Her eyes flashed blue fire. "Or even if you truly think that I am his mother, not some other woman you encountered in your travels—"

"You can't palm this off on some other woman, Rebecca, so don't even try," Jack warned.

"Fine, I won't try to explain anything to you," she said, just as furiously. "But in return I want something from you, too, Jack Rourke."

Jack had the sinking feeling her request was going to be impossible to fulfill. "What?" He bit out the word, then emotionally braced himself for the worst.

Rebecca stomped nearer. "I want you to take your adorable little baby and leave this farm and all of Blair County forever, so I can forget my reckless affair with you ever happened!"

"YOU BROUGHT NO EGGS in with you," her grandmother reproached the moment Rebecca walked in the door.

Rebecca went straight to the kitchen sink and began washing her hands. "Jack Rourke can gather them and bring them in."

Her grandmother walked back and forth, baby Andy swaddled in blankets and cradled lovingly in her arms.

Ruth paused by Rebecca. Rebecca looked down at the baby in her grandmother's arms and just for one second felt her heart catch in her throat. Andy was a beautiful baby. And now that she looked at him closely, she even thought she could see some resemblance to Jack...in the straight nose and the pronounced line of his cheekbones. Andy's hair was several shades darker than Jack's and curly where Jack's was straight, but those qualities could have come from Andy's real mother...whoever she was.

Noticing Rebecca's gentle perusal of him, Andy gurgled in delight and beamed a toothless smile up at her. Rebecca smiled back. As always, when around a baby, her yearning for a child of her own intensified mightily. And Andy, bless his little heart, picked up on that, too. His smile broadened and his big blue eyes telegraphed a willingness to be held by Rebecca, too.

"Do you want to hold the baby?" her grandmother asked.

Rebecca thought about what Jack Rourke would make of that and shook her head.

"You don't like Jack Rourke much, do you?" Ruth said.

Rebecca shrugged. Her grandmother had always been able to see far more than she wanted her to see.

If Jack stayed, her grandmother would realize there was something between them, or had been, Rebecca amended hastily to herself. "I hardly know him," Rebecca said.

Maybe it was foolish, but she much preferred to keep her mistakes to herself, and loving Jack had been a mistake. His crazy story about the baby, his showing up here now, proved that. Dear Lord, did he actually think she would give her own child away? Perhaps, had Jack been willing to listen to reason, she would have explained that to him. But one look at his face and she had known—now that he had a baby he suddenly wanted her back in his life. Not because he loved her and couldn't live without her, but because he thought Andy needed a mother. And that, she knew, was no reason for them to get together. No reason at all.

Ruth continued to study Rebecca. "It's not like you to be rude to someone, Rebecca," she chided softly.

Rebecca felt her jaw thrust out stubbornly as she struggled to contain the temper and quick tongue that always threatened to get the best of her. "I just don't think he should be here," she said finally.

"Better Jack Rourke be here, where we can watch over him, than out roaming around the countryside at will," Eli said, walking in to join the two women. "A young man that handsome and charming would have no trouble at all seducing our young women, I am afraid."

He's already done that, Rebecca thought mournfully.

"Does your dislike of Mr. Rourke have anything to do with what happened in Florida?" her grandfather asked gently.

Rebecca felt her spine stiffen. "I thought we had agreed we weren't going to talk about that anymore."

Her grandfather tucked his hands around his suspenders. "Normally you know I would not bring it up."

"But Jack Rourke is English, too," her grandmother added gently, coming around to pat Rebecca on the arm. "And you seem abnormally uncomfortable around him. We thought, perhaps because of the memories of Wesley..."

Her grandmother didn't finish, but then, she didn't have to. The memories of her time in Florida were largely bad ones. But that didn't mean they had to dwell on them now, Rebecca thought fiercely. Always an intensely private person, she found she was even more so now. "I don't know what it is about Jack Rourke that gets under my skin exactly, I just know he does," she said, not bothering to mask her temper.

Eli frowned. "I suppose someone should check on Jack and the hens."

Not me, Rebecca thought fiercely. She was not going to be alone with Jack Rourke again.

"No need for that," Jack said cheerfully as he appeared in the kitchen door, his shoulders reaching from one side of the portal to the other. He had two baskets with him, each brimming with a surprising number of brown-shelled eggs. He looked at Rebecca, challenge sparkling in his eyes, but his voice was pleasantly mild as he asked calmly, "Where should I put these?"

Darn him for taking the egg-gathering in stride, Rebecca thought. She had hoped it would make him turn and run. "In the sink, for washing," she said with a bright smile, mocking his relaxed tone to a T.

Eli cast a look out the window, at the increasingly dusky sky. "I'll see to the rest of the stock," Eli said. He left via the back door.

Ruth looked at Jack. "I noticed a moment ago that your baby needs changing. I'd be glad to do it. Where are the diapers?"

"In the bag I brought with me," Jack said.

He pumped water at the sink, and washed his hands in the cold water. Seconds later, Ruth and Andy exited. Jack and Rebecca were alone once again. He lounged against the sink beside her, deliberately standing too close. "How many more tests am I going to have to pass?" he asked.

He's not ever going to give up, Rebecca thought as she inhaled the brisk wintry scent of his after-shave. A shiver of excitement went through her. She had been pursued by boys ever since she could remember, but never like this. Never so intently. "About a million and a half," she said tartly, refusing to let the way he was pursuing her now, after nearly a year's absence, go to her head.

"Just want you to know I'm looking forward to it," he quipped. "And one more thing."

Now he was setting conditions, Rebecca thought mournfully. "What?"

Jack's gaze darkened, just the way it had before he'd kissed her, but this time he kept his hands, and his lips, to himself. "Keep in mind I give back as good as I get," he whispered softly. "This isn't over, Rebecca, not by a long shot."

Chapter Three

"Do you need any help preparing Andy's baby food?" Ruth asked as the last-minute dinner preparations were made.

"Thanks," Jack said as he stirred formula into the rice cereal specially made for infants, and then placed it in the hot water warming dish, next to the apple sauce already warming, "but I think I've got it."

He had certainly impressed her grandparents with his parenting know-how, Rebecca thought. "You seem to know a lot about taking care of babies," she said.

"I baby-sat my psych prof's son while I was in college," Jack said. He plucked Andy out of the cradle and joined the others at the table. Eli said grace. Conversation resumed, with Jack taking the lead.

"There's a lot about the Amish I still don't understand," Jack admitted as he tied a bib around Andy's neck, and tossed a hand towel over his shoulder. "For instance, is shunning still practiced in your church? And is it really as cruel a punishment as it sounds?"

Rebecca fixed Jack with a quelling gaze from beneath her lashes. She wanted him to stop this right now. Unfortunately he was so busy getting Andy settled on his lap so that he could feed him, he didn't seem to get her message. Or maybe, Rebecca thought, Jack just didn't want to get her message.

"First of all, Jack," Eli said matter-of-factly as he ladled mashed potatoes onto his plate, "shunning is not so much a punishment as an attempt to bring the sinner back to the fold."

Rebecca swallowed hard as she busied herself spooning beef and noodles onto her plate. She was not sure how she was going to make it through this entire meal, never mind the entire night, if Jack didn't stop playing master detective in search of a clue.

"What kind of sin are we talking about here, Mr. Lindholm?" Jack asked as he spooned cereal into Andy's mouth.

Jack frowned as Andy pushed half of the cereal back out again with his tongue. Jack caught the excess with the edge of the spoon, and pushed it right back into Andy's mouth. This time, Andy swallowed it, and then smiled as if the cereal tasted great.

"Are we talking about stealing?" Jack continued as he gave Andy another bite. "Murder? Coveting another man's wife?" Jack paused long enough to look briefly at Rebecca. "Not honoring the wishes of one's father and mother?"

Next, Rebecca thought, Jack was probably going to bring up the sin of making love to someone other than one's marriage partner. Just what she needed to make this whole miserable, thrilling, exciting day complete.

"You are blunt, aren't you, Mr. Rourke?" Rebecca said sweetly as she ladled lima beans onto her plate.

Jack paused and waited until she looked at him. When she did, he returned her gaze evenly. "I guess I am blunt, but I don't know any other way of ascertaining the truth," he said quietly as he looked deep into her eyes, his words imparting his secret strategy.

"And I do want to make sure I understand the Amish before the filming of my new screenplay is finished," Jack continued as he gave Andy another bite of apple sauce, "while there's still time for me to rectify any mistakes *I might have made last spring,* while I was researching and writing the first draft."

Rebecca's heart pounded as she again caught the double meaning of his words. What did he mean by rectify, anyway? Was he really here to marry her because of a baby that wasn't even hers? Or did he just want another brief fling with her, one that was every bit as passionate as their last had been? Recalling what a powerful effect his kisses had had on her before, she turned her glance away from Jack and his adorable little baby. She couldn't let herself be ruled by her emotions or her attraction to this very sexy Englishman.

Ruth smiled at Jack and said, "Your attention to detail is laudable. So many writers have painted us as a backward society, without talking to the New Order Amish such as ourselves, as well as the Old Order Amish. Our community is much more progressive in our thinking."

"I can see that, just by your willingness to accept me into your home," Jack said. "So back to the shunning, is it still practiced?"

"To a point, yes. We don't force a member out of the community, though. Rather, we work with them to try to put them back on the right path," Eli said.

Jack looked reassured by that, Rebecca noted dispassionately. "What if a woman had a baby out of wedlock?" he asked her grandfather matter-of-factly as he gave Andy another spoonful of rice cereal. "What would happen then?"

Eli shrugged, and said, just as serenely, "She would either marry the baby's father, or give up the baby to an Amish family to raise. And then she would go on with her life, and one day marry and have a family of her own."

"I see," Jack said as he shifted Andy a little higher in his arm.

"But that rarely happens," Eli continued with a fatherly complacence that had Rebecca squirming in her seat. "We keep a good eye on our young women. And couples tend to marry early, when they are still in their teens in most cases."

"The Amish are a loving, nurturing society, Mr. Rourke. Not a cruel one," Ruth said gently.

Rebecca saw him sizing up her family and knew he believed that about the Lindholms, at least. "Still, giving up a baby would be hard," Jack said, after a moment, as he gently wiped Andy's mouth.

"No harder than raising a child on your own," Rebecca interjected quickly, afraid of what might be revealed inadvertently if Jack kept this up. Lowering her lashes slightly, she gave him a look that told him quite frankly to cease this line of questioning here and now.

Jack ignored her. With Andy still on his lap, he began to eat his own dinner.

"What happened to Andy's mother?" Ruth asked. "You didn't say, Jack."

Rebecca tensed. Jack caught Rebecca's expression, frowned, then said, "She left me."

"After the baby was born?" Ruth gaped.

"Before Andy was born, actually."

"Are you divorced?" Eli asked.

"We were never married," Jack admitted reluctantly. "I would have married her, had I known about the baby, but she didn't tell me she was pregnant."

"How did you find out about the baby?" Ruth asked.

"The baby's mother left Andy on the doorstep with a note advising me to own up to my mistakes. I'm trying to do that," Jack said.

"Any chance you'll get Andy's mother to marry you now?" Eli asked.

Jack cast a casual look around. His gaze lingered briefly on Rebecca as he said, "I'm hopeful everything will get worked out and that we'll be a family, but only time will tell."

Rebecca caught her breath as her grandmother began doling out slices of apple pie. Jack was a fool if he thought he could get his way so easily, Rebecca thought, pressure or no pressure.

"When will that be decided?" Ruth asked.

Deciding too much time had spent dawdling, Rebecca got up and began to clear the table. Another mistake. As soon as she was on her feet, Jack's eyes were following her around the room.

"In a couple of weeks," Jack said, leaning back in his chair so that Andy was snuggled against him and the fabric of his corduroy shirt stretched across his broad shoulders and the hard muscles of his chest. Unable to help but look at him as she came back to the table for another stack of dishes, Rebecca could almost feel Jack against her as he had been that night, skin to skin, all hot and taking, urging her on...

Oblivious to the licentiousness of her thoughts, Jack shifted Andy a little higher, so Andy had a better view of the adults around him. "What happens if a young person decides to leave the Amish faith these days?" Jack asked. Rebecca knew he was trying to find out what would happen if she left with him.

"We don't like to see our young people leave the faith, but it happens, even in the best of families," Eli said. He and Ruth exchanged a look full of both shared memories and compassion. "In fact, it even happened in ours. Rebecca's mother married an Englishman and she lived in Ohio most of her adult life."

"And you allowed this?" Jack asked, surprised.

"We didn't have much to say about it," Eli answered Jack with a shrug. "Every young person has to decide for his or herself whether to stay or to go. Our daughter Elizabeth chose to leave the faith." Just as I did, Rebecca thought.

"It didn't mean we didn't love her," Ruth added gently as she got up to help Rebecca clear the table.

"She came to visit from time to time," Eli said.

"And wrote often," Ruth said.

"So how did Rebecca end up here?" Jack asked, his interest in her past intense.

Again, Rebecca fought a flicker of unease, that in his determined probing Jack might find out things about her she'd rather he not know, now, or ever. She faced him with a brisk, purposeful smile. "Ruth and Eli took me in when my parents were killed in a car accident," Rebecca said shortly, in a way that let Jack and everyone else know the subject was closed for discussion. Anticipating his next question, she sent him a quelling look. "And I was happy to be here."

Jack shifted Andy to his other arm. He regarded Rebecca silently for a long moment, then turned to her grandmother. "When I was in town, I saw some young Amish girls running around in tennis shoes, instead of the usual plain black shoes. Is that allowed?"

Ruth nodded. Passing by Andy, she chucked him on the chin and was rewarded with one of Andy's delighted smiles. Ruth held out her hands. Andy lurched toward her happily, and Jack, looking grateful for the respite, handed him over.

"Young people are encouraged to make their own decisions about clothing as well as their faith," Ruth said as she walked Andy around the room, patting him gently on the back all the while. "We encourage them to dress plain and simple of course, but a little rebellion at that age is to be expected."

"I see." Jack looked at Rebecca, as if wondering if her night with him had been just a simple act of youthful rebellion on her part.

Wordlessly Jack stood and carried his own plate to the sink. Rebecca had already used the old-fashioned pump to half fill the sink with cold water straight from the well outside, but she had to heat the rest on the stove, and as she waited for it to heat, she railed at the impractical side of the Amish way of life. Self-reliance was great, but honestly what was wrong with a little dependence on some sort of water heater—even a solar generated one—if it sped up their chores?

"What did you do when you were a teenager?" Jack asked Rebecca.

Rebecca turned her back to him, feeling guilty about her rebellious thoughts. It wasn't up to her to question the validity of their community's ways. She continued watching the water in the kettle on the huge black wood stove with more than necessary care. "Nothing out of the ordinary," she said. And that was true, as far as her life here in Blair, Pennsylvania, had gone.

Despite the utter blandness of her words and her noncommittal expression, Jack saw through her evasive statement. To Rebecca's dismay, he leaned against the sink, folded his arms in front of him and continued to prod her mercilessly. "You didn't ever want to leave or break free of the constraints here? Sorry," he said, lifting a hand in a gesture of goodwill to both Ruth and Eli. "I mean no offense. I'm just curious, because I know teenagers rebel, no matter what circumstances they live in. It just seems to be a normal part of growing up."

"Indeed it is," Ruth agreed with a cheerful smile. Seeing Andy was beginning to be a little restless, she went over to get him a rattle.

"So I was wondering how Rebecca handled it," Jack continued easily as he slanted Rebecca an appreciative glance. "She seems to be a strong-minded young woman."

"She is at that," Eli agreed. He, too, glanced at her and smiled. "But she came back to us, like we knew she would," he concluded with familial pride.

"Back?" Jack asked pleasantly, his dark blue eyes sparkling as if he had just picked up on some extraordinarily interesting tidbit about her. "Where was she?"

"I was in Florida," Rebecca answered swiftly before either of her grandparents could say a word. Grabbing the pot holders, she carried the heavy pot of boiling water to the sink and carefully added it to the soap and water there. "I took a job as a maid in a bed and breakfast there when I was seventeen."

Jack had moved back to allow her room to work. Now he closed in on her again. His brisk masculine scent stirred her senses in a disturbing way, and lent a rubbery feeling to her knees. Rebecca drew a silent breath, telling herself to calm down. He was only a man, after all. And she had been around men all her life. She could handle this, if she just kept her emotions—and her temper—tightly reined.

"Why did you go so far from home?" Jack asked softly, still watching her carefully.

Because I was a fool, Rebecca thought, the steam from the sink rising to bathe her face.

"We wanted her to see more of the world, before she decided whether to go or stay," Eli said, answering for her.

Jack looked at her again, his gaze narrowing attentively. Rebecca had the feeling he was learning more than he let on, not just about her, but her entire family. Knowing what havoc his interest in her could cause made her heart pound.

"And you came home?" he said.

"The following year," Rebecca replied, keeping her gaze averted. But it was too late. She had already noticed how sexy he was, with his thick chestnut hair all rumpled, and the faint shadow of evening beard now lining his stubborn jaw.

"Was that when you married?" Jack asked.

"About the same time," Rebecca said as she slipped on a pair of rubber gloves and began to wash the dishes, again with more than necessary care. She would get through all Jack's questions, all his probing, and then Jack would leave. He would take his baby with him and forget about her; they'd both go back to their normal lives. As if nothing had ever happened. All she had to do was get through the next few days.

"And it can also be necessary sometimes, especially for young people like Rebecca, to do something different from time to time," Ruth added, still walking Andy around. "That's why she went to Indiana last summer to work at a bed and breakfast in Indiana."

"How long did you work there?" Jack asked Rebecca, his dark blue eyes filled with sudden interest.

"A few months," Rebecca mumbled, wishing fervently the subject had never been introduced.

"Longer than that," Eli corrected, like the stickler for detail he was.

Ruth nodded. "You left in June and came back right after Christmas. Remember, Rebecca?"

Again, Jack's face lit up.

The clock struck six in the adjacent living room. "Oh, dear," Ruth said. "You're going to be late for your singing tonight if you don't hurry," she said.

Seeing an escape route from Jack, Rebecca hurriedly added more dishes to the soapy water in front of her. "Don't worry. I'll be quick," she promised. And then I'll leave.

Again, Jack looked intrigued. "I've heard about singings, but I've never been to one," he said, then probed her with a decisive yet innocent look. "Mind if I tag along?"

Rebecca knew what Jack was up to now; he wanted to ask her about her stay in Indiana. She was about to say, "As a matter of fact, I do," when her grandmother interrupted.

"That's a splendid idea!"

"But—" Rebecca sputtered, the last of her dishes scrubbed and put on the drainboard to dry.

"I will take care of the baby," Ruth said as Andy beamed up at her adoringly.

"Great." Jack smiled victoriously at Rebecca. "Then it's all set."

A shiver of anticipation and unease went through Rebecca like a lightning bolt. Darn it all, she did not want to be alone with this man.

"I'll hitch up the buggy," Eli said, getting to his feet.

Jack smiled at her grandfather. He, too, reached for his coat. "I'll come with you," he offered and followed Eli out the door.

"WHAT'S WRONG, REBECCA?" Ruth asked gently the moment the men had left.

"Nothing," Rebecca fibbed. She hated lying to her grandmother but she couldn't tell her the truth, either—that her grandparents had just given Jack information that was going to have him jumping to conclusions and asking all kinds of questions. "I'm just worried about being late for the singing."

"Worried about being late, or worried about being alone with Jack Rourke?"

Rebecca turned away, wishing she had never been so foolish as to sleep with Jack Rourke. "You heard how nosy he is," she complained. "Asking questions about everything, personal questions."

Ruth nodded as she continued to pace back and forth, Andy in her arms. "You don't want him to know about your past."

Rebecca shrugged, not above confessing to this much. She met her grandmother's glance. "I'd rather he didn't."

Ruth patted an increasingly drowsy Andy on the back. "Jack seems like a nice man," Ruth said.

Rebecca frowned. She knew she couldn't come on too strongly here or her grandmother really would suspect something was up. "There's no doubt he's handsome and charming. But it takes more than being handsome and charming to be a good man."

"You distrust him?" Ruth studied Rebecca bluntly.

Rebecca reached up and checked her hair. As she had suspected, a few errant strands had escaped her kapp. She tucked them in as best she could and tried not to think about the loving, gentle way Jack had sifted his fingers through her hair both before and after they had made love, as if her hair were the finest treasure he had ever found.

Finished restoring order to her hair, Rebecca clamped her lips together. "I don't want to talk about this."

Ruth looked down at Andy, who was almost fast asleep in her arms, then back at her granddaughter. "Is there something your grandfather and I should know?" she asked quietly.

Rebecca looked down at the sweet, innocent Andy and shook her head. It was killing her to know that Jack had slept with another woman sometime either shortly before or after he had made love to her... and to know that other woman had had Jack's baby and then abandoned Andy. What kind of woman had Jack slept with, anyway?

Not that it mattered now, Rebecca thought, since she was out of Jack's life, and had been for some time. But Rebecca couldn't confide any of that in her grandparents. Knowing how they had suffered with her both before, during and after her disastrous marriage to Wesley Adair, she had since made a firm practice of keeping her mistakes to herself. She wouldn't veer from that course now. It was enough that she'd had a fling that had turned her own world topsy-turvy. She wouldn't let the same happen to the people who loved her most, too.

Swallowing hard, she forced herself to put on a cheerful front. "No. I am just in a mood," she explained with a rueful wave of her hand, and a woman-to-woman look. "It's probably just the time of year. I'm tired of the snow, anxious for spring." And anxious for Jack to leave.

Chapter Four

"You had the baby in Indiana, didn't you?" Jack said as he helped Rebecca into the covered black buggy. "That's how you managed to keep it a secret."

With a decisive snap of the reins, Rebecca started the horse on the way. "Good theory, Jack. Only there's one problem with it. Where was Andy when I returned to Blair County right after Christmas?"

"How should I know?" Jack settled back in his seat. "Maybe you brought him with you and secretly cared for him here at the farm."

"Then why didn't my grandparents put two and two together and know you were the father the instant you showed up at the farm, Jack? Why didn't they read you the riot act, if that were the case?"

Jack frowned. Rebecca had a point. "So maybe Ruth and Eli didn't know about the baby or the pregnancy. Maybe you arranged for someone else, someone in Indiana, to care for Andy."

"Then how did Andy end up on Alec Roman's doorstep?" Rebecca asked scornfully, looking even more beautiful in the moonlight filtering down through the trees than she had inside the house.

"I don't know." Jack shifted restlessly in his seat as the buggy bumped along the paved road. "Maybe you changed your mind and decided to make me own up to my mistakes. Maybe you wanted me to come after you."

"Oh, absolutely," Rebecca agreed dryly. "I really wanted my quiet life here disrupted, my grandparents shocked, hurt and dismayed, my reputation ruined."

Jack frowned. "So I can't figure out exactly how you think—yet. I will."

Rebecca shook her head. "That'll be the day," she murmured beneath her breath. With every bounce of the buggy, she seemed to slide a little closer to the middle of the seat and to Jack. "How much farther?" Jack demanded as she slid toward him a little more and they finally made contact from hip to knee. Sitting this close to her was agony.

Rebecca slanted him a quelling sidelong glance. "Another five miles or so."

Five miles! Jack scowled. He had wanted to be alone with Rebecca, but not like this, freezing to death in an unheated Amish buggy, without even a lap robe to keep them warm. He regarded her meditatively, unable to help but admire the competent way she handled the reins. "You're still angry with me for showing up here, aren't you?" he said softly, wishing with all his heart that she wasn't, because if she wasn't so angry, maybe she would be more willing to talk honestly and unreservedly with him. But he also knew that Rebecca had every reason to be annoyed with him. By invading her home, he had overstepped his boundaries. Of course she was mad.

Rebecca lifted her eyes heavenward. "Your keen skills of observation amaze me," she remarked drolly.

He ignored the reproach in her voice and pointed out politely, "You know, it would have been faster to take my car." And more comfortable, too.

Rebecca slanted him yet another sassy look from beneath her thick golden lashes. "Being from Los Angeles, I would think you would appreciate the environmental soundness of our ways. Or perhaps you like smog?"

Most of the Amish Jack had encountered during his research expedition last summer had been blissfully ignorant of the world outside their own. Not Rebecca. "You sure know a lot about the world for an Amish woman," he drawled, finding he would do just about anything to hold her attention, even if it meant baiting her almost continuously. As for the true story of what had happened while she was in Indiana last summer and fall, he would have to wait until she trusted him completely before he'd have those questions answered.

Rebecca concentrated on the winding road ahead of them. "My downfall, I am sure. The other," she added tartly, "was ending up in your bed."

Jack smiled. "Ah, so you do remember," he murmured in delight. Leaning closer, he regarded her with a comical leer. "I was beginning to wonder."

Rebecca gripped the reins a little tighter. "A night like that would have been hard to forget," she said in a strangled tone of voice.

"Impossible to forget," Jack corrected. He leaned forward, pressed his lips to the back of her hand, and felt her tremble. "The memories of that night have been driving me wild the past few days, Rebecca."

"What happened that night was a foolish mistake," Rebecca shot back as she jerked her hand away, the hurt in her low voice as palpable as her scorn. "We have to forget we ever behaved so recklessly."

"Even if there's now a baby involved?" Jack asked.

"That baby isn't mine, Jack, and if it weren't for Andy, you wouldn't have come back for me at all."

Jack was silent.

"It's true, isn't it?" Her voice was thready with hurt. "You're only here because of the baby."

"I thought that was what you wanted, for me to get lost and stay lost."

"It was!" Rebecca insisted, color flowing into her cheeks in a way that made her delicate bone structure all the more pronounced.

"But just because I abided by your wishes doesn't mean I stopped thinking about you, Rebecca. I've thought of you more times than you'll ever know. But I respected your privacy and your different way of life and I stayed away, until Alec found Andy on his doorstep. And then I had no choice. Andy needs his mother every bit as much as he needs me."

"But I'm not his mother!" Rebecca protested.

"So you keep saying."

Her light blue eyes narrowed on him in a way that made him decidedly uncomfortable. "And you keep not wanting to believe it's true," she said.

Jack shrugged, not about to back down now that he'd come this far. "I know what I feel in my heart, Rebecca, but you're right. We shouldn't keep talking about Andy's parentage, since that always leads to heated discussion. Let's talk about each other instead. While we were out hitching up the horse, Eli told me you were never so glad to come home as when you came back from Florida."

"So?"

Jack ignored the irritation in her voice. He continued to probe. "Eli made it sound like you regretted ever going there. I just wondered why. Were the working conditions bad?"

"No. They were fine."

"Then what didn't you like about it?" Jack persisted.

Rebecca shrugged. "I missed my family and friends here. We wrote letters to each other, of course, but it wasn't the same as being here and visiting and going to weddings and seeing the new babies born and weathering every hardship together and sharing every joy. I felt cut off from all that in Florida," Rebecca continued softly, a faint note of reverence and appreciation creeping into her tone. "There's a closeness of family and community here that doesn't exist out in the English world."

"Maybe you just didn't meet the right English people, Rebecca. I have plenty of very nice, very caring friends in California."

He watched as Rebecca transferred the reins to her right hand, and used her left to draw her thick black wool cloak closer to her slender form. She must be as cold and uncomfortable right now as he was feeling.

Rebecca glanced at him. "What about you, Jack? Are you close to your family?"

Jack thought about all the things he and Rebecca still had to learn about each other. "I never knew my father. He didn't stick around long enough to marry my mother." Crazily enough, that fact still hurt and angered Jack, even though he'd had years to deal with his abandonment. "As for my mother," Jack continued, picking his words carefully, "she died several years ago, so it's just me these days. Or at least it had been until Andy came along. Now I've got family again, a child to love. And I couldn't be happier about that, Rebecca. It's what I've wanted for a long time."

"Then I'm happy for you," Rebecca said in a voice that sounded thick with suppressed emotion, but sincere, too. "And I'm sorry about your mother," Rebecca continued softly, surprising Jack even more. She reached over to grip his hand tightly in hers. "I know how hard it is to lose a parent."

Jack squeezed back, and then released her hand reluctantly. "I guess we have that in common." Hers was a small gesture of comfort, but one he appreciated.

Looking ahead, he saw they were approaching a sprawling farm. Several other buggies were coming from the opposite direction. Another cluster of buggies was already parked in the yard, in front of the plain white frame house. "What's going to happen next?" Jack said, as Rebecca guided the horse to a halt.

"We'll go inside," Rebecca said. Jack stepped down from the buggy then reached up to lend her a hand. As he helped her down to the ground, they were flanked by two young men—Jack estimated them both to be in their early teens—in Amish garb. They looked Jack over, taking in his leather bomber jacket, corduroy shirt, jeans and running shoes. "What have we here, Rebecca?" the taller one asked.

"A friend," Rebecca said. "This is Jack Rourke. He's staying with my family. Jack, I'd like you to meet Levi and Dieter Hoffer. They're family friends. I've known them forever. They're like my little brothers."

"Not so little anymore," Dieter corrected, proudly sticking out his chest. "We're fourteen."

And definitely feeling their oats, Jack thought. He could tell by the dancing lights in their light blue eyes that the two were already plotting some sort of mischief for the evening.

"Nice to meet you both," Jack said.

"Nice to meet the latest Englishman who is sweet on Rebecca," Levi said with a wink. Both boys laughed. Rebecca flushed with embarrassment and glared at Levi until he and Dieter took her not so gentle hint and ran off.

"What did he mean by that?" Jack asked.

Rebecca avoided Jack's eyes altogether as she shook her head in silent aggravation and dismissed the comment with a wave. "The boys are just at that juvenile age where they think it is great fun to annoy me until I lose my patience."

"Does that happen often?"

"Sometimes. Not to worry." She gave Jack a significant look. "I get them back, when necessary."

Jack grinned. This was a side to Rebecca he hadn't seen before. "How?"

Rebecca leaned forward and spoke in a confidential whisper. "One day not too long ago when they were being particularly pesky, I played a reciprocal prank on them."

"What'd you do?"

Rebecca smiled smugly. "I told them I saw a moose in the woods by the covered bridge."

Jack frowned. "I didn't know there were any moose out here."

"There aren't." Rebecca grinned, delighted with her roguery. "It took Levi and Dieter almost an hour to discover the curious tracks I'd laid were false and that they'd been sent on a wild moose chase. They've been trying to get back at me ever since."

"Get back at you?" Jack asked.

"By embarrassing me, what else?" Looking unconcerned by the teenage boys' antics, Rebecca took Jack's arm just above the elbow and urged him toward the house. "Come on. We're going to be late for the singing."

Jack enjoyed the blending of voices as he and Rebecca stood shoulder to shoulder among the other young, single people there and sang the lively German hymns. The hymn singing was followed by refreshments and a square dance in the barn. Jack had just linked arms with Rebecca when Levi passed by again. "Better watch yourself with the Englishman, Rebecca," he warned, suddenly only half joking. "You know what happened before—"

"Levi." Rebecca glared at him like a chastising older sister. "Cut it out. I mean it." Giving Levi no chance to comment, Rebecca grabbed Jack's arm and dragged him off in the direction of the dancing. Wordlessly she tugged Jack out onto the middle of the barn floor. Not about to waste the opportunity to have her in his arms again, Jack swung her round and round to the invigorating tune the group of Amish fiddlers were playing. It had been cold in the barn when they'd first entered, but now, with the dancing and the crush of people, it was warming up fast. Just as he was.

"So what is it you don't want Levi to tell me?" he asked, flattening his hand possessively against her waist. He saw the temper flare in her clear light blue eyes.

"Nothing," she said.

Jack tightened his grip on her, determined to get to the bottom of this mystery whether she helped or not. "Try again."

She smiled at him cantankerously. "I will not."

"Then I'll ask Levi myself," he said, and started to release her.

Rebecca gripped him, hard. "That won't be necessary, Jack. Levi is just teasing me."

And pigs read books. "About what?"

"My...looks." Her floundering for an answer gave her away more than the pink color creeping up her throat, into her jaw.

"What about your looks?" Jack asked. Then, as the dance ended, he took her hand and led her resolutely over to a bale of hay stacked against the far wall, sat down and pulled her down beside him.

Rebecca smiled out at the dancers, looking to all the world as if she were enjoying herself. "My hair gets very white in the summer. It always seems to attract a lot of attention from the summer tourists."

"There are plenty of Nordic blondes in this part of the country, Rebecca."

"True," Rebecca said as she tapped her foot to the beat of the music. "And it happens to other young single women here, too. Englishmen see us. The next we know, they are taking our pictures. Trying to talk to us. Lure us on dates with them."

Levi was talking about more than just gawking tourists; Jack would bet his life on it. Something had happened to Rebecca. "So?" he said.

"So the young Englishmen seem to think that just because they are drawn to us that we are drawn to them." She glared at him rebelliously as the fiddlers began another spirited song. "They are wrong," she said flatly.

The double-edged meaning of her words did not escape him. And though he knew she wasn't telling him the truth, at least not all of it, he also knew he wasn't going to get any more out of her now.

"So what are you going to do about Andy when you return to L.A.?" Rebecca watched as Levi and Dieter joined the dancing, too, leaving her and Jack the only two people on the sidelines. "Now that you know I won't be coming with you and the baby."

Jack shrugged. "I'll raise Andy by myself."

"You make it sound so easy," Rebecca lamented softly.

"And you make it sound so overwhelming," Jack replied.

"That's because it is an overwhelming prospect to me. I don't know that I could manage a baby all on my own, particularly if I had no family around to help out, and I had to earn a living, too. That's a lot to take on, Jack."

Jack shook his head. She was making too much of this again. "I've got a job that allows me to work at home ninety percent of the time, and enough money to pay a good nanny to help out when I need help. If all else fails, I'll take some parenting classes, too. One way or another, Andy and I will get along."

He was really determined to do right for his son; Rebecca obviously found that very appealing. Jack began to relax. Maybe things would work out between them after all.

"When are you going to tell Andy about his mother? When he's old enough to understand?" Rebecca asked.

Jack shrugged again. "Hopefully I'll have convinced his mother to marry me and live with us by then."

"And if you haven't?" Rebecca asked.

Jack grabbed her hand and pulled her through the shadows, and back, into the tack room. It was as dark as night. Jack pushed her inside, moved her back against the wall and took her into his arms. "Come back to L.A. with us, Rebecca, and we'll never have to worry about that. Andy will already have us both, watching over him and loving him."

Rebecca closed her eyes; she looked like he had just offered her the impossible. "Oh, Jack," she whispered in obvious dismay. "Jack, don't—" Her breath caught as he molded his body to hers.

"I want you," he said, lowering his head and brushing his mouth across hers. "I've never stopped wanting you."

Rebecca gasped as he kissed her again, hard. Jack knew he was going too fast but he couldn't help it. Being with her seemed to bring out the caveman in him. All he wanted was to make things right between them. He was ready to make amends, to court her properly, if she'd let him. "I want to start over with you, Rebecca. Please, say you'll give me another chance, for Andy's sake. For ours."

Rebecca paused. She wanted to start over with Jack, to begin again in a more conservative, normal way. But she was afraid for so many reasons that it was already too late. Sooner or later Jack would realize what she already knew: that she was not Andy's mother. And then, Rebecca thought, he would want to find Andy's real mom and reconcile with her.

She had walked away from Jack once. That had been hard, but it hadn't been nearly as difficult as it was going to be for her to walk away from him now that he'd come back into her life once again and she'd gotten to know him a little better.

"Just think about it," Jack urged gently as he slowly, reluctantly released her. "You don't have to give me an answer now."

That was good, Rebecca thought, because she didn't have an answer for Jack. The only thing she knew for certain was that the more she was around him, the more she wanted to be around him.

Jack spent the rest of the evening propped up against the barn wall, watching Rebecca dance with other Amish men. No matter how much he looked at her, he couldn't get his fill. Rebecca was beautiful, incredibly beautiful, in the plain clothing. And very popular with the young Amish men. But he couldn't help but remember how she had looked with her hair down, waving gently, as thick as silk . . . the heavy fragrant weight of it spread over his pillow.

He felt his body tighten painfully. How long, he wondered, before she was back in his bed where she belonged? How long before he could convince her to marry him? It wasn't as if she had never lived English before. It wasn't as if her grandparents wouldn't understand; they would. All she had to do was tell them she loved him. But first, he would have to get her to trust him again. After that, admitting she loved him would be easy.

Around ten, the dance ended. Goodbyes were said and coats and bonnets gathered. Jack escorted Rebecca out to the buggy. He could tell by the way she avoided looking him in the eye, and the stiff set of her shoulders that she was still confused and on edge.

Jack conceded silently that she had a right to be upset with him for kissing her in the tack room. Anyone could have walked in on them and carried the news of their kiss back to the community. It wasn't like him to be so reckless and shortsighted. But that, too, was going to change, Jack promised himself silently. For every moment he spent with Rebecca was a moment invested in his and Andy's future. He wanted his son to have a mother.

He climbed up into the buggy after her and while she was getting settled, he took the reins.

"What are you doing, Jack?" Rebecca pivoted to gape at him. "You don't know how to handle a horse, never mind one reined to a buggy."

Out of his peripheral vision, Jack could see both Dieter and Levi loitering next to their two buggies, watching Jack and Rebecca quarrel over the reins. There had never been a better time to assert his mastery over the situation, and not so coincidentally, over her. Besides, maybe it was time he stopped trying to convince Rebecca to return to the English way of life with him, and instead concentrated on showing her that they all could live in both worlds with equal chances of making a successful go at becoming a family.

"You know, you're right," Jack teased Rebecca gently, "it is time I learned how to handle a horse." Fortunately Jack had paid enough attention to what Rebecca was doing earlier, to be able to start the horse up and turn it toward the lane. Once that was done, the horse fell into line behind the other vehicles heading toward the road. "And a woman," Jack continued glibly, "if the jokes Levi and Dieter were telling about me every time they thought I was out of earshot tonight are to be believed."

Rebecca flushed and sat farther back in the buggy. She folded her arms in front of her defensively. "You're talking nonsense, Jack."

Jack only wished that were the case. "Am I? This is a patriarchal society. Maybe if I'd been more masterfully dictatorial with you in the first place, Rebecca, you never would have left me the morning after."

Rebecca leaned forward, checking both ways as they headed out onto the main road. "If you'd been any *more* dictatorial, I never would have stayed with you that night."

Satisfied, she leaned back in her seat, keeping more to her corner of the buggy than she had en route there. Jack didn't need a crystal ball to know why. The way she kept raking her teeth across her lower lip told him she was thinking about their kiss in the back of the barn. . . maybe wanting another one, somewhere en route home?

Jack was glad to see Rebecca direct him to take the road north, when almost everyone else was going south and west. He guided the horse through the turn, holding the reins just as he'd seen her do. When they were headed straight again, he settled back in his seat and asked what had been on his mind for what seemed like forever. "Why did you stay with me that night, Rebecca?"

Rebecca folded her arms in front of her. "I don't know."

Jack wasn't buying her innocent act. Beneath that demure Amish clothing beat the heart of a very passionate woman. She might say she still wanted nothing to do with him, but the way she'd returned his kiss tonight said otherwise. "Yes, you do," he disagreed gently.

She held herself so still for such a long moment that he thought she wasn't going to answer. Finally she shrugged and said softly, "The whole night seemed a little unreal to me, like something out of a story someone made up. I knew how much you desired me and I got caught up in those feelings, all right?" She lifted her chin and glared at him. "I was a fool to behave so recklessly!"

Jack shook his head. "No, Rebecca, you weren't a fool to love me."

"If I hadn't, I wouldn't be in this mess right now."

Jack tugged on the reins and brought the horse to a halt. The moon was so bright, the terrain so flat and wide open, that anyone within a mile of them would've seen them stop, but he didn't care. He turned to face her, his knee nudging her thigh in the process. "What mess?"

"Your chasing after me, invading my home." She started to reach for the reins, but he wouldn't let her have them. Instead, he wrapped his left arm around her waist and hauled her against him, so she was half sitting on his lap.

"You know what I think, Rebecca?" Jack whispered, dropping the reins altogether so he could slip his free hand between her black bonnet and the side of her face. She gasped as he gently caressed her cheekbone. "I think you resented my reappearance into your life at first, but now that you've seen how much I already love our son and could love you, given even half a chance, I think your feelings have changed. I think you want me to chase after you," he said, kissing her temple, and then her nose, her chin, her ear. As she trembled in his arms, he drew back just enough to look into her eyes again. "And you know what else? You kiss me like you *want* me to catch you again, too!"

Rebecca sucked in her breath and flattened both her hands across his leather jacket. Her eyes were huge, her lips parted softly, her breathing erratic. "Jack, Jack, don't—"

Her voice was like velvet, sliding over him, drawing him in deeper and deeper. He tightened his arms around her, wanting her so badly. "Don't you get it, Rebecca?" he whispered, all the longing he felt for her pouring into his low voice. "I'm here because I want you back in my life. I don't want another brief fling with you, but a chance, a fair chance this time, at forging a real relationship with you, as two parents who are as committed to being good and kind and decent to each other as they are to loving their son."

"Oh, Jack," Rebecca said in a voice that was choked with emotion. Her eyes welled up, too.

"Tell me you want Andy to be happy, and loved, by two parents," Jack commanded gruffly.

"I do," Rebecca said.

"Then that's all I need to hear." Jack bent his head and kissed her again, tenderly this time, and with every ounce of restraint he possessed. If he did more than that they were going to end up making love right here and now. And that they couldn't do. He'd already put her through enough.

With a sigh, he released her slowly and picked up the reins. She sat back in her corner of the buggy, a look of utter confusion on her face, and released a shuddering breath. "You're making me want to be Andy's mother, do you hear me?" she whispered.

"I hear you," he said, smiling. And that was exactly what he wanted to happen.

They'd barely gone another half mile when the sound of rapid hoofbeats and the clatter of wooden wheels on rough pavement sounded behind them. The buggy had no rearview mirror so Jack had to stick his head around the canvas side to see what was going on. To his amazement, two black Amish buggies were coming at him, hell for leather.

"What the—" he muttered, his irritation getting out of hand as quickly as the buggies were gaining on them.

"Don't panic, Jack," Rebecca said. Their horse, hearing the commotion coming up right behind them, spooked and took off at such a breakneck pace that both Jack and Rebecca were knocked back in their seats. "It's only a buggy race."

Only a buggy race? "They could have at least waited until we got out of the way," Jack said. He spared a glance at the deep ditches on either side of them, the covered wooden bridge up ahead, the flat terrain speeding past.

Knocked sideways, Rebecca fought the back and forth jolting of the buggy and struggled to sit up. "They're racing *us,* Jack. And I told you not to panic!"

The buggy hit another rut, jolting them so hard that Jack lost his grip on the reins and dropped them. One flopped outside the buggy and dragged along the ground. Rebecca lunged for it just as they approached the bridge. She caught it, and managed to stop their runaway horse, just as the other two buggies overtook and then blocked them. Jack wasn't at all surprised to identify the drivers of the other two buggies: Levi and Dieter. Of course. He knew the young teens had been yearning to get into mischief all evening.

"Saw your buggy stopped. Been doing some sparking on the way home, Rebecca?" Dieter teased, with a bratty younger brother type of wink.

"Ja," Levi drawled, "we thought there might be some problem."

"No problem," Rebecca lied smoothly as she straightened her spine. "I was just explaining to Jack the fine points of driving a buggy."

"Ja, well, the first thing you perhaps should explain to him is how to hold on to the reins," Dieter teased with a chuckle, then clicked to his horse and headed off in the opposite direction. Levi turned his buggy behind them. The two continued to lead their horses and buggies back and forth, in front of and behind Rebecca and Jack. To Jack's amazement, Rebecca seemed to take the boyish harassment in stride. "This foolishness doesn't bother you?" Jack asked.

Rebecca met his eyes and again handed Jack the reins. "Young Amish men are known for their pranks. It's generally referred to as 'cutting up' and it's the way they let off steam. They're just horsing around. They probably thought I was driving, when they came up behind us like that. They know that I know how to handle a horse. I've had carriage races with them before."

Jack's frown deepened as he anticipated the rest. "Who won those races?"

"I did, of course."

"Of course," he mimicked dryly. "But that still doesn't excuse the way they spooked our horse and nearly forced us off the road."

"Perhaps it doesn't," Rebecca said with another uncaring shrug, "but it's still a better way for a young man in his prime to let off steam than seducing young women.''

Jack slanted her a glance. ''I didn't seduce you, Rebecca,'' he reminded her flatly, as Levi and Dieter finally gave up and Jack was able to start their horse off on the path back to the Lindholm farm once again. ''You came to my bed willingly.''

For a moment, she was very still, neither arguing nor admitting to his claim. ''It is time we got home,'' she said quietly, looking as afraid to risk her heart as Jack was afraid not to risk his. ''That baby of yours will be wanting his father.''

Chapter Five

"It's a good thing I bought you a couple of those blanket sleepers before we left Philadelphia," Jack told Andy several hours later that same evening. "Because it's cold in here tonight."

Andy's tiny brows knitted together, as if he were concerned about the situation, too.

"I also should have asked how to work the wood stove before everyone went to bed," Jack continued, speaking quietly so as not to wake the others.

Andy's brows rose again in silent question. He waved a fist in the air and cooed. "Trying to tell me you're hungry, aren't you?" Jack soothed as Andy clumsily aimed his fist at his mouth. Finally latching onto it after the third pass, Andy sucked noisily on his fist. "Well, not to worry," Jack continued, "ye olde midnight snack is on the way. There's only one small problem. I don't have the slightest idea how to heat this bottle for you."

Andy blinked and took his fist from his mouth. "We don't even have hot running water I could set the bottle in," Jack murmured. "And I hate the idea of waking anyone else up at this time of night."

"Too late," Rebecca said softly, from behind him. "You already woke me up."

If she was still upset with him for the way he had kissed her, both at the barn dance and after, she wasn't showing it. She seemed more amenable to their becoming friends. And that, Jack thought, was a start. Encouraged, Jack smiled at her. "What about your grandparents, are they awake, too?" Jack asked.

"No." Rebecca avoided locking eyes with Jack by gazing tenderly down at Andy instead. Basking in her obvious admiration, Andy immediately beamed her back a toothless smile, then giggled and cooed. Rebecca bent and pressed a kiss to Andy's tiny fist. She smiled again, then reluctantly released his hand.

"But then," Rebecca continued as she gave Jack a cursory look, "my grandparents sleep more soundly than I do." She brushed past him. "I'll stoke up the fire for you."

"Thanks," Jack said. Andy still cradled in his arms, he followed Rebecca to the wood stove. Rebecca's gentleness with Andy appealed to Jack on a very fundamental level. And she appealed to him physically as well, never more so than at that moment. She was wearing a high-necked, long-sleeved white flannel gown that swept the floor. She had tied a navy shawl around her shoulders for warmth. Her hair was down and she wasn't wearing a kapp. She had never looked more beautiful, and he had never wanted her to be part of his life more than he did at that moment, not just in a fleeting, physical or practical sense, but in a more permanent way, as the mother to his son.

Flushing slightly under the intensity of Jack's gaze, Rebecca opened the stove door and added several small dry logs to the fire. Jack watched as she added water to a small pan and put it on the burner, and then set Andy's bottle down inside the pan. "It'll take about two minutes to heat."

"Thanks. I'm sorry we woke you. I don't know why he's awake."

Rebecca tossed Jack a wry look that made her seem even prettier. "Andy's probably hungry," she said, moving close enough to gaze tenderly down into Andy's face. Andy blinked up at Rebecca, then began to smile as if he not only recognized her, but welcomed her gentle, feminine presence.

Jack leaned against the kitchen counter, enjoying the cozy scene. Being with Rebecca this way seemed meant to be. "I meant Andy doesn't wake until three o'clock now, if we put him to bed at ten. At least, he didn't at Alec's," Jack said. Jack frowned as he shifted a squirming Andy higher in his arms, then patted him gently on the back. "I think he realizes he's in a strange place."

Rebecca nodded, looking distinctly uncomfortable with the intimacy between them, an intimacy that appeared whenever they were together for any length of time. She glided away from Jack, the voluminous white flannel gown she wore doing nothing to hide the enticing roundness of her breasts, the slenderness of her waist, the enticing flare of her hips, or the sleek, slender lines of her thighs.

Just watching her, Jack felt his body tighten. He knew she wanted him. He'd felt it in her kiss, in the way her body instinctively softened against his whenever he held her in his arms. He didn't understand why she wouldn't surrender to that desire, to the inevitability of their being together. He didn't understand why she wouldn't admit they'd had a child together, so they could go on with their lives, become a family. What was really holding Rebecca back? Maybe it was time he dug a little deeper and tried to find out how Rebecca felt about being a mother, period.

"Then again—" Jack met Rebecca's long-lashed gaze straightforwardly "—maybe where Andy and I are doesn't have anything to do with Andy's wakefulness at all. Maybe he just wants his mother." Holding her gaze, he stepped even closer, so she could inhale Andy's fresh baby scent, and he could surround himself with the sunny, springlike scent that was Rebecca. "Why don't you hold him?"

Rebecca blinked, then stepped back and away. "I don't think so," she said, edginess in her voice giving her away. She stepped past him, removed the bottle from the pan and tested the formula on her wrist.

Unable to take his eyes from her, Jack moved a little closer. The heat from the stove that emanated around him did nothing to alleviate the aching he felt in his loins. "Why not hold him? He doesn't bite. Not yet anyway."

Rebecca handed Jack the bottle of formula. "I'm not afraid of Andy, Jack," she said tersely, even more color flowing into her cheeks as she dropped her gaze, inadvertently sweeping the front of his pants, then lifted it back to his face. "I just don't see any reason to get close to him."

"Why not?" Jack studied her delicately boned face as he gave Andy his bottle. "What are you afraid of?"

Rebecca moved to the far side of the kitchen. "You," she said in a voice barely above a whisper.

Beneath the gown, Jack could see her nipples tighten. "Why would you be afraid of me?" he asked, as his body tightened more in response.

Rebecca paced back and forth, her silky blond hair flying out around her shoulders. "Because you want what you want without any thought to the future or to the consequences."

"You're wrong about that, Rebecca. I've given the future and the consequences a lot of thought, and it'd be a crying shame for Andy to have to grow up without a mother, and a real home."

Rebecca folded her arms in front of her defiantly and whirled to face him. "That's not my problem, Jack."

"Isn't it?"

Her bare lip thrust out stubbornly. "No, it isn't."

Jack closed the distance between them in a few smooth steps. He offered her the nursing baby. "Just hold Andy, Rebecca, just for a moment."

She shook her head and kept her arms clamped in front of her. "Your plan is not going to work, Jack.

Andy is adorable. But my affection for him is not going to make me fall in love with you.''

Jack studied her in growing frustration. ''Why can't you at least give us a chance?'' he whispered.

''Because I have a life here, Jack, a good life, with grandparents who love me unconditionally.'' Her pretty jaw tightened. The air between them crackled with suppressed physical energy. ''I'm not going to mess that up.''

Jack quirked a brow. ''Your grandparents seem very understanding to me.''

''Trust me.'' Rebecca glared at him. ''They wouldn't understand about our night together in Philadelphia, and I won't hurt them that way.'' She brushed past him, the silkiness of her hair catching him in the face. ''Now, if you'll excuse me, I'm going back to bed.''

After she had gone, Jack settled in the rocking chair next to the fireplace in the living room. He sighed heavily as he looked down at the innocent baby in his arms. ''Well, Andy, I guess she told us. She doesn't want us back in her life. Not that you should take this personally, you understand. It's not that Rebecca doesn't love you, or couldn't grow to love you, you understand. Just that she's afraid right now, and to be perfectly honest, so am I.''

Jack paused, shifting Andy in his arms. Noting Andy was starting to get a little squirmy again, Jack sat Andy up so he could burp. While he patted Andy gently on his back, Jack continued to explain the situation. He didn't know how much of this Andy was getting, but he knew he felt better just talking about it.

"So much in my life has changed in the past few days. Prior to Alec's call last weekend, all I had in my life was my work." Andy gurgled, and Jack turned him around to face him, so they were looking at each other, man to man. He smiled fondly down at his son. "Now all I care about is finding a way to bring your mom back into our lives without causing her undue heartbreak and shame in the process."

Andy finally burped and Jack settled him back into the curve of his arms. He began giving him his bottle again. "Considering the fact that having a baby out of wedlock is still treated as a problem here, rather than the badge of honor it is in Hollywood, we've got our work cut out for us."

"WELL, ANDY, looks like we're having soup for the noon meal," Jack remarked the next day as he walked into the kitchen and found both the Lindholm women hard at work.

Ruth looked up from the chopping board. "Indeed we are. How did your visit with Cornelius Glassenheit go?"

"Fine. I learned a lot about the ninety different types of Amish buggies currently being made. Choosing a new one must be as difficult as choosing a new car."

Ruth smiled at him indulgently while Rebecca worked pointedly to ignore him. "Would you like a cup of coffee or some sugar cookies as a morning snack?''

"Thanks, but I think I'll just sit here in the rocking chair and watch how the two of you go about your daily chores, if you don't mind.''

"Not at all,'' Ruth said, though Jack could tell at once by the tense set of Rebecca's shoulders that she minded his presence in their kitchen a lot. Ruth wiped her hands on a plain white dish towel, and looked around. "Oh, my! I forgot the carrots! I better go down in the root cellar. Rebecca, do we need anything else while I'm down there?''

Rebecca smiled at Ruth. "Not that I can see, Grandmother,'' she said in the soft, deferential voice she always used around her grandparents.

"I'll be right back.'' Ruth tossed the words over her shoulders as she hurried to the cellar stairs. Her heavy black shoes clunked as she made her way down.

Alone with Jack, Rebecca glared at him. With Andy in his arms, Jack moved closer to her, watched as she filled the old-fashioned wringer washing machine with warm sudsy water and clothes that needed laundering. Once they were in, she moved a lever back and forth to work the agitator.

"Why don't you use one of the gasoline-powered washing machines?'' Jack asked. He had seen some in his visits to other Amish homes, the previous spring.

"Because it would be foolish to spend money on one when this works just fine.'' Rebecca leaned over the washer, rinsed the clothes one by one, using the hand crank that activated the wringer.

Jack knew this was the way the Amish did things, and part of him even admired the Amish's self-sufficiency, but another part of him, the creative part, resented it. Rebecca was a talented designer. The variety and beauty of her quilts proved that. She could be working full-time on her quilts, if she didn't spend so much time doing chores that could easily be done completely by machines.

"Will you stop that?" Rebecca hissed as she put the last of the clean clothes through the wringer.

"Stop what?" Jack asked. Aware Andy had gone to sleep, he put him in his cradle and tucked a blanket around him.

"Stop watching me," Rebecca hissed at him under her breath as she passed by Jack, a laundry basket braced on her hip.

She looked so provoked, he couldn't help but tease her. "Why, when you're so pretty?"

"I am not."

"Oh, yes you are," Jack said, and he meant it. Rebecca might be dressed plain, but the blue chambray dress with the round collar, and long sleeves, and full, fitted skirt, the black apron, did for her figure what a designer gown did for Michelle Pfeiffer. He was even beginning to like the kapp she wore on her head, though he still preferred her hair down, the way it had been last night.

Rebecca scowled at him. She put her laundry basket down, next to the back door, and then returned to the washer to start a second load of clothes. "We both know the only reason you are still here is to bother me, not to research your movie.''

''You think so?''

''I know so!''

Her words should have made him feel guilty. They didn't. Maybe because Jack knew his motivations here were noble, even if Rebecca did not. He wanted to own up to his responsibilities. He wanted to do right by her and Andy. If only she would let him. ''Well, it's just too bad you don't want me here,'' Jack whispered back as he put his hand next to hers and moved the lever back and forth to work the agitator on the washer for her. ''Because I'm here to stay.''

Rebecca glared at him from beneath her thick blond lashes. She removed her hand from beneath his, stepped back slightly and smiled up at him sweetly. ''I'm sure you'll give up eventually and go away.''

Jack held her stormy blue gaze. ''Don't count on it.'' He was rewarded with another glare, followed swiftly with the sound of footsteps on the stairs. Ruth came up, three large carrots in her hand. ''Think this'll be enough?'' she asked Rebecca.

''Plenty.'' Rebecca smiled at her grandmother as she went to retrieve another clothes basket.

''I want to hear more about this story you are writing, Mr. Rourke,'' Ruth said. ''You said last night it was about a Robert and Jill—''

Jack smiled as Rebecca returned with an empty basket and set it down beside the washer. ''Romeo and Juliet.''

"Yes." Ruth nodded encouragingly, then frowned her dismay. "I did not understand that remark."

Noting the clothes were clean, Jack began transferring them to the adjacent rinse water, one at a time. "Romeo and Juliet was a play by Shakespeare. It was written a long time ago and is very famous. In it, two young people fall in love, but their families don't approve of the match and they come to a tragic end."

"Oh, dear. I hope your story does not come to a tragic end."

Jack slanted a glance at Rebecca who was taking the clothes he was rinsing, and putting them through the wringer. "Not if I can help it."

"Is your story set in modern times?" Ruth asked as she peeled the carrots with slow, arthritic movements of her hands.

"No." Jack shook his head as Rebecca left his side and disappeared into the pantry. "It's a turn-of-the century historical romance about the love between an English con man on the run and an Amish girl."

"You know a lot about con men?" Rebecca asked, innocently enough, as she emerged from the pantry, a big bag of wooden clothespins in her hand.

Jack finished the rinsing and put the last of the clean clothes in the laundry basket, just as Rebecca had done before, with the first load of laundered clothes. He straightened slowly. "Not so much, really. But I've got a lively imagination and I can see how a people that were so pure of heart could be taken in by someone not so pure," he said. Finished with the laundering, he dried his hands and rolled down the sleeves of his burgundy corduroy shirt.

Rebecca stomped to the door and reached for her black wool winter cloak. "We Amish are pure of heart, not naive."

Jack followed her to the coatrack and shrugged on his leather jacket. "I never said you were naive, Rebecca," he corrected softly. He helped her on with her cloak, his hand brushing her slender shoulder inadvertently. "Still, I can readily see the inherent problems in an English-Amish romance and how falling in love with an Amish woman would change a man forever."

Her cheeks flushed, Rebecca shrugged away from him and bent to pick up a load of the wet clothes. Jack started to follow her, then stopped. It bothered him to see Ruth struggling with the soup on a day when the arthritis in her hands was clearly acting up, just as it bothered him to see Rebecca washing clothes in a wringer washing machine. He turned to Ruth.

"You know, I have a food processor, an electric cutting devise that swiftly grates cheese and slices vegetables, that could do all that in three minutes." Jack paused, not wanting to offend, yet needing to ask. "Doesn't it ever bother you, knowing your life could be a lot easier than it is? That you could do things faster, without so much labor?"

"Not really." Ruth shrugged and offered an accepting smile. "But then, I've never lived any other way than this." She looked at her granddaughter sympathetically. "I know it's different for Rebecca, since she lived English until she was ten."

Jack looked at Rebecca, who was suddenly not looking at him. "I'm going to take these clothes out and hang them on the line to dry," she said, and slipped out the door.

Jack looked at Ruth. "If you'll keep an eye on Andy for me, I'll give Rebecca a hand."

"Of course I will." Ruth smiled at Jack.

Jack picked up the other basket of damp clothes and went out to join Rebecca at the clothesline that ran across the yard at the rear of the Lindholm home. The day was sunny, and unseasonably warm for February, the temperature almost up in the forties. "I can do this by myself," Rebecca said stiffly.

"I insist." Aware his heart was pounding, Jack asked, "Why didn't you ever tell me you lived English until you were ten?"

Rebecca shrugged and kept her glance averted. "You never asked."

"You knew I assumed differently." His anger, already simmering, began to boil. He didn't understand how Rebecca could give so much of herself, physically, to him, and so little, emotionally. For him, the two things had always gone hand in hand.

Rebecca didn't so much as blink in the face of his anger. "So?"

"So," Jack explained, working hard to contain his feelings of betrayal and hurt, "all along I've been thinking that you would have to live a whole new life in order to be with me and Andy, only to find out it's not such a sacrifice for you at all. That you've already lived a great part of your life as an English person!"

She grabbed him by the front of his jacket and pulled him farther back into the rows of freshly hung clothes, so they were concealed from sight. "Look, Jack," she whispered fervently, her fear of discovery obvious, "I never said I didn't feel half English. You just *assumed* my parents died when I was very young, because no one said otherwise when the subject was brought up briefly at the dinner table last night. You just assumed that I had no memories of living English, that I only recalled living Amish. But that's not true, okay? I do remember a lot of things, like...going to the mall to get a new dress, talking on the phone to my other third-grade friends, having a dishwasher and a washing machine and everything else that goes with that kind of life!" That said, she started to let go of his shirt.

He caught her hand with his, and held it, inside the front of his jacket against his chest. Now that she had finally started to open up to him a little, he wasn't going to let her just run off.

"It must have been hard for you, losing your parents and having to make such a drastic life-style change all in one fell swoop," he said softly, his heart going out to her and all she had been through as a child.

Rebecca swallowed, looking briefly undone by the compassion she heard in his voice and saw in his eyes. "Yes," she admitted to Jack. "It was hard, at first.

Very hard. But my grandparents loved me and were very understanding of how difficult it was for me to have to live without hot running water and so forth after always just having it, and so given time...I adapted.''

''Why didn't you tell me that last night?'' Jack asked, hurt that she hadn't found some way to work at least a little of that information into their conversation.

''Because I didn't want to discuss it, that's why, and certainly not at the dinner table, when my grandparents might take something I said about the frustrations I feel sometimes about Amish life the wrong way and get their feelings hurt.'' Rebecca tugged on her hand, reeling back slightly when Jack let her go. ''Besides, I learned a long time ago that people think what they want to think. And it's not up to me to correct any misconceptions you might have about me, Jack!''

Jack held the clothespins for her while she resumed hanging up the clothes. He studied her. Part of him was very glad the gloves were off, and they were speaking with gut-wrenching honesty at long last. ''That's not why you didn't tell me,'' he drawled.

Looking slightly flustered, as if having him stand directly next to her damp underclothes embarrassed her, Rebecca planted both her hands on her slender hips and challenged, ''Then why didn't I tell you?''

That was easy, Jack thought. ''Because you didn't want me to know how much more we had in common than I initially thought,'' he said.

Rebecca picked up a pair of Eli's black trousers. "We have nothing in common," she seethed.

Jack reached around her deliberately to apply the clothespins this time, trapping her deliberately between his body and the wet clothes. "Says who?"

Rebecca ducked beneath his outstretched arm, the soft swell of her breasts bumping his arm in the process. "Says me!"

It was all Jack could do at that point not to drag her into his arms and give her some of the tender loving care Rebecca was so sure that she did not need from him. "What about our baby?"

Rebecca whirled on him so suddenly her kapp fell halfway off her head. Flustered, but no less angry with him, she reached up to catch it with one hand. "I don't care what kind of mess you've gotten yourself in, Jack Rourke, I am not going to take responsibility for that child, and that's final!"

Jack could understand her walking away from him last spring. After all, they'd been strangers who had just met, from different parts of the country. They'd had completely different life-styles. But the baby they'd made changed everything. They had a responsibility here. To his continuing disappointment, she refused to see it. "If that's the case," he said in a low accusing voice, "then you really are a heartless wench!"

Her temper exploding, she lifted her hand to strike his face. Jack caught her hand before it could connect with his skin. Exerting pressure, he forced it down between them. Her display of passion was more encouraging than she knew, he thought in silent triumph. "Maybe you're more English than you think, Rebecca," he taunted softly, determined to get her to admit her feelings. He tightened his grip on the silky soft skin of her wrist as she started to struggle. "A real Amish woman would never strike anyone, no matter what they said or did."

Rebecca stilled and regarded him coolly. The ice maiden again. "You would try the patience of a saint, Jack Rourke, and I am no saint," she said quietly.

Jack's frustration with her mounted. His lips curled bitterly. "How well I know that."

Rebecca stepped on his foot, deliberately. "I want you out of here!" she said.

Jack accepted the punishing weight of her foot with stoic grace. "And I told you before, I'm not leaving, not until you own up to your responsibilities," he countered, then ever so slowly, ever so reluctantly, let her go.

For a second, all was still between them. Jack felt the winter sunshine beating down on his head. He heard the soothing sounds of the country... the gentle neigh of a horse, the flapping wings of the chickens in the barnyard, the slow, gentle whir of the windmill next to the barn.

He could see the pulse beating madly in her throat. See the fear and the desire and yes, even the pain and the loss, in her light blue eyes.

For another long moment, Rebecca continued to stare at him grimly. Wordlessly she spun around on her heel, picked up the empty laundry basket and marched into the house. Jack picked up the other basket and followed behind her. Whether Rebecca wanted to admit it or not, he had gotten to her this morning. And that was the first step.

Chapter Six

"Don't forget the soup for Mrs. Yoder," Rebecca said, following her grandmother and grandfather to the door, a quart jar brimming with homemade vegetable soup in her hand.

"We'll be back before dark," Eli promised as he added the soup to the basket of home-cooked food Ruth had already packed.

"I'll have supper ready and waiting," Rebecca said. "Jack can help me see to feeding the animals. And tell Mrs. Yoder I hope she is feeling better soon."

"With your grandmother's homemade soup, who wouldn't be?" Eli teased. His hand on her grandmother's shoulder, he escorted Ruth out the door.

Rebecca turned to see Jack leaning over Andy. He had just taken off one disposable diaper and put on another. She watched as he quickly snapped Andy back up into a clean warm sleeper. Unlike most of the Englishmen she had met, Jack was a man who was very comfortable around babies. It seemed there was nothing he didn't know how to do. She admired that about him, just as she admired the kind, respectful way he treated her grandparents.

Jack lifted Andy out of the bassinet and held him against his broad chest. Watching Andy bounce his tiny fist off the muscular chest, Rebecca felt a thrill of desire surge through her, and center in the most womanly part of her. Although she had tried to forget, she could still recall all too well what it was like to be held against that hard male body of his. He not only knew how to love and care for a baby, but he also knew how to love and care for a woman, too. And that made it doubly hard for her to turn away from him, but turn away she must.

"You know we could wash diapers for Andy while you're here, if you like," she said inanely as she went hurriedly back into the kitchen.

Jack followed her lazily, Andy still in his arms. He didn't stop until he was close enough for her to smell the spicy scent of his after-shave, or notice how closely he had shaved. He grinned laconically, his dark blue gaze drifting down to her mouth before returning to her eyes with determined male intent. "I don't figure on being here all that long," he said softly.

Rebecca's breath hitched. Needing something to do—anything was better than being mesmerized by Jack's sensuality—she filled the teakettle and put it on the back burner. Her back to him, she repressed the hurt the thought of him leaving brought and remarked casually, "I thought you were staying until I agreed to be Andy's mother."

Jack followed her as she moved restlessly over to the tea canister. "I don't figure that will take all that long, either," he said softly.

He was standing so close to her, she could feel the heat and tension in his tall, strong body. She whirled to face him. Her back against the counter, she stared up into his face with unmitigated frustration. "Then you figure wrong," she said flatly.

Jack transferred Andy to his other shoulder. "Do I now?" he asked, the challenge in his low tone unmistakable. Rebecca's heart raced. Their eyes held.

"My growing affection for Andy has nothing to do with what's going on here, Jack."

"Doesn't it?"

Rebecca looked into Jack's dark blue eyes and felt herself begin to tremble. She knew she wanted him to kiss her again and knew he wanted that, too. Swallowing hard, she looked away. Andy gurgled, muttered something unintelligible, and made a clumsy grab for the collar on Jack's corduroy shirt.

Jack tore his eyes from hers and beamed like a father whose child had just won the Nobel prize. "Hey, did you hear that?" he said. "Andy just said a word."

Rebecca measured tea into the china teapot. "He did not."

"He did, too. Say it again, Andy. Say 'play' for Rebecca. Come on, be a sport for daddy and say 'play...play...'"

Andy beamed a toothless grin up at Jack and mumbled something that did sound a little like play after all, Rebecca noted with equal parts admiration and exasperation. "See?" Jack crowed triumphantly. "He said it again. He's a genius!"

Not wanting Jack to get too carried away and give the baby a swelled head before he was even out of diapers, Rebecca lifted her eyes heavenward. "You have some imagination, Jack."

Jack put Andy down in his infant seat, strapped him in and then closed his hands around an infant-sized rubber rattle. "My imagination, hmm?" He put the infant seat on the center of the big kitchen table, so Andy had a good view of the kitchen, then sauntered toward Rebecca.

He took her by the shoulders and held her in front of him when she would have bolted. "I'll tell you one thing I didn't imagine, Rebecca," he said in a low soft voice that sent shivers of awareness coursing through her at a madcap rate. "I didn't imagine the chemistry between us or what happened that night last April..."

Another thrill went through her, this one more potent than the last. She had known when Jack showed up in Blair County that there was going to be trouble. And that feeling had been confirmed the moment she had looked into his boyishly handsome face. "Jack, please—"

Jack's palms slid down her arms, past her wrists. He captured her hands in his and linked fingers with her in a very intimate way. "Who's going to hear us, Rebecca?" he taunted her softly. "Your grandparents are gone. Andy can't exactly tell anyone what we're saying, even if he did give a hoot, and—" Jack cast a look over his shoulder at Andy, who was busily inspecting the rattle in his hand "—I don't think he does."

Rebecca drew a shuddering breath and, gathering all her courage, lifted her face to his. "You're talking nonsense, Jack," she reprimanded sternly.

His dark blue eyes only darkened more as he took her into his arms and held her against him. "Our feelings for each other aren't nonsense, Rebecca," he said, taking off her kapp and tugging down her braids. He sifted his fingers through her hair, freeing it in exactly the same way he had the night they'd first met and made love. He gazed down at her tenderly. "We both know we felt something special that first night we met," he whispered fervently, lowering his mouth to hers, kissing her sweetly, lingeringly. "We still feel that way, whether you admit it or not."

Her lips tingling, her senses awash in sensation, Rebecca pushed him away. She couldn't, wouldn't, let herself dwell on the rightness of his body pressed up against hers. "No, Jack," she said breathlessly, recalling the easy way he had let her go... until he erroneously thought he had a child with her. "We don't."

But Jack was not to be dissuaded. "Don't we?" he countered softly, pulling her close again, so close that their bodies fit together like pieces of a puzzle, hardness to softness, maleness to femaleness. He threaded his fingers through the hair at her nape, and forced her head up to his. "Then tell me why it feels so good when we kiss."

He touched her face with the back of his hand, caressing her from the uppermost curve of her cheekbone to her chin. He rubbed his thumb across her lower lip, stared deep into her light blue eyes. "Do you know I still remember the way you felt against me that night, all soft and warm and giving? And I think about the way you looked when you were in my bed." His hand glided down her throat, over her collarbone, to the uppermost curve of her breasts. "How the sheet draped your soft, womanly curves—"

Rebecca's breasts tightened into aching pinpoints of pleasure. "Stop it!" She pushed away from him.

He moved in behind her, wrapping his arms around her waist, clamping his palms together at her navel. Her buttocks were nestled in the hard curve of his hips. Lower still, she could feel the swelling evidence of his desire. There was no denying he wanted her as much as she wanted him.

"You were naked that night, Rebecca," Jack whispered, trailing his lips through the softness of her hair. She turned her head sharply to the side. His lips trailed lower, to the exposed slope of her neck. One hand stayed locked around her waist. The other moved up, inside the black cotton apron, to cup the swell of her breast through her sensible blue dress. Her nipple hardened even more.

"Wonderfully naked and you let me carry you up to my bed and take all your clothes off and make wild passionate love to you." Without warning, he turned her swiftly around to face him. "And no amount of denying it on your part is going to make those memories go away."

She shoved away from him, hard, her whole body throbbing. "That night was a mistake!"

"Was it?"

Rebecca was saved from having to answer that by the whistling of the teakettle. Her shoulders stiff, she marched to the stove, slipped on a quilted oven mitt and carried the kettle to the counter. There, she added steaming water to the teapot, and put on the lid to let it steep.

Jack waited until she had finished. The moment she had, he came up behind her again, wrapped his arms around her waist and kissed his way down her neck. "Don't run away from me, Rebecca," he urged softly, his hands sweeping down her hips, over her thighs and back up again, to the most womanly part of her.

Rebecca twisted in his arms, afraid if he touched her there she really would be lost. She wedged her arms between them, for protection. "I have to."

"No, you don't." He looked down at her, his expression brimming with tenderness and passion. "I can take care of you," he whispered fervently. "We can be together, you and me and our baby."

"For the last time, Jack, Andy is not my baby!"

"What are you telling me?" he asked, his voice clipped.

It hurt Rebecca to say the words, but she knew they had to be said. Jack had to start facing the truth. "I'm saying," she said flatly, "that baby belongs to you and another one of your women. Not me."

"If Andy doesn't belong with you, then he doesn't belong with either of us, Rebecca."

"How do you know that?"

"Because there hasn't been anyone else in my bed, Rebecca. Not for a long time."

Rebecca wanted to believe that. But the facts said otherwise. Someone had left Jack that baby, telling him to own up to his mistakes. Jack's willingness to assume responsibility for his son, the easy way Andy and Jack had bonded further substantiated the claim. If it were true, it meant Jack had been with another woman, in roughly the same time frame he had been with her. And that hurt. Still, curiosity made her want to listen to his defense. "Why not?" she asked tersely.

Jack shrugged. "It doesn't matter." He bit out the words, his expression closed and unreadable.

Rebecca busied herself getting down the plain white teacups and saucers. "I think it does."

Jack's jaw turned rigid. "You want to know my romantic history, is that it?"

"It seems to me you've certainly done enough prying into my life."

Silence fell between them. Not caring if the tea was properly steeped or not, Rebecca sloshed some in two cups and carried them to the table. Jack followed her. Seeing she wasn't about to give up on her quest for information, he turned a chair around backward, sat down opposite her and hooked his arms over the back of it. "Okay, there's never been anyone serious in my life."

Rebecca sat primly in her chair and folded her hands on her lap. As the silence strung out between them, she sized him up quietly. "Why not?" she asked in a tight, clipped voice. She picked up her tea and sipped. It was very hot and too weak.

"Because it was just never right, that's why," Jack said gruffly, looking her in the eye. "There was always something missing and I knew it. I felt it in here." He palmed his chest emphatically.

Rebecca took another sip. She knew he meant the words to comfort her. But in truth, they did just the opposite, because they told her a reality she had been dreading, that Jack was the type of man who drifted from one highly romantic affair to another. No doubt he moved on as soon as the passion faded. "Then you must also feel that I am no different from the others," she retorted simply, testing his devotion.

Jack released a quick, impatient breath. "Wrong, Rebecca," he said shortly. "You are different."

"Why? Because I'm Amish?" The bitter words just slipped out.

"Because you're you."

Her face burned. Her eyes were hot and dry. Inside, she just felt empty, scared and afraid. Afraid because she knew how easy it would be for her to drift into a dead-end love affair with Jack. Besides, what kind of relationship could they have if he wouldn't trust her? How could she possibly get involved with a man who wouldn't believe her when she told him Andy was not her child?

Finally she shook her head.

She knew Jack was trying to be honest with her. That didn't, however, mean he had a good grasp of the cold, hard reality of their situation, or could separate what he wanted to be from what really was. "You say all the right words, Jack," she said with a certain weary resignation. "That is probably what makes you such a successful writer."

Jack's jaw tightened. For a moment, he looked as hurt and upset as she felt. "You don't believe that I could make you happy over the long haul, do you?" Jack asked bitterly.

What could she say? There was no point in denying her reservations. No point in pretending that Jack's temporary dream could ever be a lifelong reality. Not when the only reason he had even come to her was the baby, and the baby wasn't hers. She looked him straight in the eye. "No, Jack," she said simply, "I don't."

Because if he had felt they had something even half as special as he claimed, he wouldn't have let almost a whole year go by without contacting her again.

HE SHOULD HAVE KNOWN it would happen this way, Jack thought as he fed the chickens and gathered the eggs. All the time he was growing up in Philadelphia's seamy inner city, struggling to find a way to survive, a way out, there'd been no one who had ever believed in him. He'd said he was getting out of there one day, and taking his mother—who'd worked two minimum wage jobs just to keep their heads above water—with him. His friends had laughed. His mother had wanted to believe it, but still doubted his dreams could ever come true, and that, too, had hurt.

He'd said he was going to college. His friends had laughed again. And kept right on laughing, even as he got a scholarship to one of the state's most prestigious prep schools, and gone on from there to Penn. The Ivy League university hadn't proved much easier on him, despite the support of his two best friends, Grady and Alec. Yet he'd kept going, knowing one day he would make it. He'd attended UCLA grad school. From there, had gone on to work as a junior screenwriter for one of the major studios.

Those first few years as a paid writer had been very lean indeed. For every one person who had encouraged him, there'd been ten who had told him he'd be better off selling real estate or hawking used cars than trying to make it as a writer. But he'd persisted, and eventually he made it. He'd managed to move his mother into her dream home before her death. So how had it come to this? he wondered in frustration. How had he come to be here, chasing a woman who wouldn't even admit she'd had his baby?

"Need a hand there, son?" Eli asked as Jack shut up the chicken coop and walked out.

"Thanks, Eli, but I think I'm finished here," Jack said.

"The cows—?"

"And horses have all been fed, watered and brought in for the night."

"Good job."

"Thanks."

Eli fell into step beside Jack as they headed toward the house. "Rebecca's in a mood," he said.

"Yeah." Jack sighed. "I know."

"What happened?"

Jack shrugged. What could he tell Eli? That he had tried to put the moves on Rebecca, in order to prove to her that she not only had feelings for him but still harbored a remarkable, once-in-a-lifetime-kind-of-passion for him, too, and she'd resisted? That he'd tried to talk to her, and she'd stymied his efforts there, too? None of that could be said. And yet Jack respected Eli enough to want to tell him the truth, or at least what he could of it. "She doesn't want me here," Jack admitted, finally. "I think I ask too many questions."

Eli grinned and stroked the snowy white beard that covered his cheeks and chin but not his upper lip. "It is true, Rebecca does not like questions."

Jack paused on the back steps leading into the house. "She's always been like that?"

Eli nodded and turned his collar up against the cold. "Rebecca is a very private person."

So Jack had noticed. "Is she able to talk to you and Ruth, at least?"

"Sometimes." Eli frowned. He stepped inside the back porch, noted the woodpile was getting low and motioned Jack back out again. Jack paused long enough to set the eggs inside the back door, then followed Eli back out again.

"We wish it were all the time," Eli continued as he headed toward the woodpile at the other end of the farmyard. "But...sometimes she has spells where she needs to be independent of others."

"Like when she went to Florida?" Jack said, hoping to learn more about this marriage of Rebecca's, and when and exactly how it had ended.

"And last year," Eli affirmed with a nod as he picked up a piece of kindling that needed to be split and set it on the stump, "when she went to Indiana. She never told either her grandmother or me what was wrong but we knew something was bothering her."

"How did she look when she came back?" Jack asked casually as he reached for the ax. Stepping up to the stump, he split the first log, then picked up the pieces and handed them to Eli.

Eli shrugged as he cradled the kindling in his arms. "Better. Healthier. Like she was eating again."

Again, Jack's heartbeat sped up as he thought about the first symptoms of pregnancy. Skipped periods. Moodiness and lethargy. Morning sickness. "She wasn't eating last summer?" Jack asked as he selected another piece of wood to split into stove-size sections.

"Not much. She said her appetite was gone. We were worried, so we made her see the doctor in town."

Jack had to struggle to keep his soaring emotions in check. He was irritated, because Rebecca had almost, *almost* had him believing Andy wasn't her baby. And he was concerned that she had felt she'd had to go through her unexpected pregnancy alone. "What did the doctor say?" Jack asked casually.

"He suggested a change of pace for her."

Nice and vague, Jack thought. Probably at Rebecca's request. "Did he tell you that?" Jack asked.

"No. Just Rebecca. And I begin to see why you might have irritated my granddaughter, Jack Rourke," Eli said with a censuring grin. "You do ask far too many questions."

"Sorry." Jack struggled to keep his emotions in check. "It's just . . ." He paused again, wanting to be as truthful with Eli as he could. "Rebecca's such a mystery to me."

Eli nodded. "Rebecca is a mystery to all of us sometimes, but that is her right, Jack. It is her way."

"You're right, of course," Jack said. There were some things that were private. He understood Rebecca's wanting to keep an unplanned pregnancy to herself. He was just sorry Rebecca had felt she couldn't come to him.

Eli continued to study him. "You wish she were more talkative about herself, don't you?" Eli prodded.

Jack gave Eli a veiled glance, then went back to splitting kindling. "I wish she felt she could trust me." *I wish she would allow me to own up to my mistakes and make a home for her and our child.*

"Perhaps she will," Eli said, "in time." He held out a hand to Jack, signaling they had split enough wood to keep the stove going for the rest of the night. Jack put down the ax.

Jack picked up his own armful of wood. "I hope she does open up and talk to me about her life here," he said. *I really hope so.* Because if she didn't, he would never get her to leave Pennsylvania with him. They would never have a chance at any kind of future, even as friends. And the thought of that was almost more than he could bear.

Chapter Seven

"Hey, did you see that? Andy reached for his rattle and picked it up all by himself!" Jack said. Excited, he called the others over to the infant seat. They all gathered around to watch just as Andy whacked himself in the nose and let out a startled, hiccuping cry.

"Whoops. Sorry, buddy." Jack picked him up and cradled him close, looking every bit the devoted father—to Rebecca's continuing dismay.

"What he needs is something soft," Ruth said, patting Andy gently on the head.

"Like a stuffed animal?" Jack asked.

"Or an Amish doll." Ruth turned to Rebecca with a smile. In a panic—she already felt far too involved with Jack and his problems as it was—Rebecca tried to ward off her grandmother's next words with a glance. To no avail. "Why don't you make Andy one?" Ruth asked.

Because that is a motherly thing to do, Rebecca thought, *and I am not Andy's mother.* But, unable to say that for the questions it would prompt, she suggested brightly, "I could, of course, but it'd be faster to buy one in town."

Eli frowned his disapproval. "Since when do we buy what we can make ourselves? Besides, those dolls are for tourists. Jack and Andy are our friends."

Rebecca was amazed at the speed Jack had ingratiated himself with her grandparents.

"Normally Amish dolls are made for a child by his or her mother, aren't they?" Jack asked, with a pointed look at Rebecca.

Her heart pounding, not so much in fear he'd give their love affair away, but fear he would try to pick it up again, Rebecca nodded. "Yes," she said tightly, and went back to finishing the supper dishes, "they are."

Ruth held out her arms to Andy. The baby smiled at her and went willingly into her soft arms. "But in the case of a child who has no mother, a friend or relative would step in to do it," Ruth continued, smoothing Andy's downy soft hair, which, Jack had noted, seemed to be getting lighter every day now. "I'd sew one myself but my fingers aren't as nimble with a needle as they used to be."

Rebecca hung up her dish towel. Clearly Jack was not going to give up on this. Besides, they still had a long evening ahead of them . . . several hours, and this would help her fill up the time. "I'll do it," Rebecca said. "In fact, I'll get started on it right away."

Rebecca went upstairs to her bedroom and knelt at the chest at the foot of the bed where she stored the scraps of clothing and bolts of fabric she used for her quilts. She quickly picked out scraps of dark blue, black and cream fabric. Jack came in behind her and admired the quilt in progress on her frame. "This what you're working on now?" he asked gently. Pale blue diamonds radiated outward from the center, in ever-escalating sizes. Within each diamond, there were collages of many colors, braided over and through one another in what at first glance seemed a random design, but on closer observation, was instead a very well-planned, very complex pattern.

"It's beautiful. What's the pattern called?"

Rebecca didn't want his praise any more than she wanted his company. But figuring it was to her advantage to keep him talking on something less personal than the two of them, she said, "It's called a Log Cabin, Barn Raising Design, and I learned it while I was in Indiana."

"Right. Last summer," Jack said.

A chill slid down her spine. Rebecca closed the top of her cedar chest, but remained where she was, kneeling on the floor in front of it. She had an idea where this conversation was going. "We've already talked about this, Jack," she warned.

"Yes, but I didn't know then what I know now." Jack knelt next to her. He put the fabric she had just taken out aside and took her limp, lifeless hands in his. "Eli told me you were moody and upset when you left for Indiana, but that you wouldn't talk about what was bothering you."

"That's right, Jack, I couldn't," Rebecca whispered unhappily. "Not without revealing what I'd done...how I'd gotten involved with you. They wouldn't have understood, Jack."

Jack clasped her hands gently. "Are you sure about that, Rebecca? Ruth and Eli seem very understanding to me."

"Somehow I just can't envision them approving of my having a tryst with a man who picked me up on the side of the road."

"How about forgive, then?"

She wrested her hands from his and rose jerkily to her feet. "You've got to stop this, Jack."

"Stop what?"

"Fantasizing. Pretending everything will go your way just because you want it to!"

He was silent, studying the heightened color in her cheeks, and the ever-escalating panic in her eyes. Rebecca could see he had already made his mind up about what had happened. "Then why did you go, if not to have the baby?" he asked curtly, careful to keep his voice low. "Why were you in a mood? Why did you lose your appetite? Why did you go to the doctor in town before you left?"

Rebecca glanced past him, to the open door, to see if anyone was within earshot. Seeing no one, hearing nothing, she turned back to Jack, stood on tiptoe and whispered, "I went to the doctor in town because my grandparents made me go. And I went to Indiana because I needed to get away."

"To have my baby?"

"No! To get my thoughts straight!" Frustration bubbled up within her. Her hands in fists, she leaned closer and hissed, "I was confused!"

"Why?"

Rebecca whirled and went to the window. She stood looking out at the farm she had grown to love. A farm that was more home to her than any other place on earth, a farm Jack would have her leave. Aware he had followed her and was now standing just behind her, Rebecca spoke in a monotone without turning around. "It bothered me, what we'd . . . done. I—I'm not like that, Jack. I don't do things like that. I didn't know why I'd responded the way I did. I needed time to think about it." She turned around to face him, her back to the windowpane. "So it wouldn't happen again."

He was silent, staring down at her. She knew she had done nothing to convince him that she hadn't had his baby during her self-imposed exile in Indiana, but she also knew that if they dallied any longer someone would come looking for them. "I've got to go downstairs."

He put a hand on her arm. "Eli sent me up to look for the checkers. He's challenged me to a match."

"Oh. They're in the next room, I think." Rebecca led the way to the bedroom next to hers. She opened the closet door. She could see the checkers but couldn't reach them. Wordlessly Jack got them down for her.

"Where's Andy?" Rebecca went back to her room for the fabric and her sewing kit.

"With Eli and Ruth." Jack paused. "I've never seen two people who appreciate children more."

"All Amish do."

He stopped her as she started to brush past him. "Hey, thanks for making the doll. I'm sure he's going to love it."

Rebecca refused to let him read anything into her actions. He was imagining far too much as it was. "We'll see."

"LOOK, ANDY, Rebecca made you a doll," Jack said an hour and a half later. Tired from their long day of work and visiting, the older couple had gone to bed at nine-thirty. Rebecca had stayed up to finish the doll and help Jack see to Andy's 10:00 p.m. feeding. Although Jack protested otherwise, she still had a feeling he wasn't comfortable cooking on the wood stove. "Isn't it neat?" Jack said.

Rebecca watched in dismay as Andy stared at the faceless Amish doll she had made disinterestedly, then shoved it away with a spastic movement of his arm and turned back to his duck-shaped blue plastic rattle.

"Andy?" Jack shook the doll back and forth, but Andy paid no attention to the replica of a little boy in a blue shirt and black pants and suspenders.

Rebecca closed the lid on her sewing basket. Her spirits, which had already been low, plummeted even further. Her grandfather was right: she was in a mood. And it was all due to Jack and the pressure he continued to exert on her. And now Andy as well.

Rebecca touched Jack's arm, took the doll and put it aside. "Let him go after the rattle, Jack. He obviously prefers it."

I can't even make a doll to please an English infant, Rebecca thought tiredly. What chance would she ever have of pleasing a thoroughly English husband like Jack in the long term? He was enamored of her now, yes, but she knew all too well how that would change once marriage vows were said and he tried to settle into a normal married life with someone like her. He would swiftly tire of her outdated Amish ways, and at the same time, she wouldn't be English enough to suit him, either.

"I'm sorry Andy hurt your feelings."

"He's just an infant. How could he possibly hurt my feelings?" Rebecca retorted.

If she was upset, and she admitted she was, it was because, being around Jack every day, she couldn't help but fantasize about what it would be like to *really* be the mother of his child. After all, it was clear Jack would make a wonderful father, and perhaps one day a wonderful husband as well. And she knew it was dangerous to be thinking this way when she wasn't Andy's mother, and never would be.

What would happen when Jack finally realized that? Rebecca wondered sorrowfully. Would he leave Pennsylvania again, without her? Or would he ask her to go back to California with him anyway so they could marry and make babies of their own? And if Jack did...was she up to that? Did she really want to leave her family again?

"Andy could upset you," Jack explained carefully, "by rejecting the doll you made for him."

Rebecca shrugged. She had accused Jack of fantasizing too much, but she was now doing it, too. "Face it, Jack, your son likes things that are shiny and plastic, not soft and cuddly."

Jack thrust his hands into the pockets of his jeans and studied her in silence. "Is that what happened before? Andy rejected you? Is that why you gave him up?"

Rebecca flushed as she went to heat the bottle for Andy. "Give it a rest, Jack."

He lounged against the kitchen counter, his arms folded in front of him. "Not until you tell me the truth."

This was like trying to move a boulder with a sewing needle. "I have told you the truth!" Rebecca protested.

Jack quirked a disbelieving brow. "All of it?"

Guilt flooded Rebecca without warning as she thought about her marriage. Jack still thought she was a widow. She'd done nothing to correct that mistaken assumption because she didn't want him to know about the terrible humiliation she'd suffered by getting involved with another Englishman. "Look, you can handle the bottle for Andy. I'm going upstairs now."

He caught her arm just above the elbow, as if they were square dancing, and swiftly reeled her in. Her full skirts swirling around her legs, she collided with the hardness of his chest. His body was just as immovable as his will. Even through the layers of clothing, she felt the beginnings of his desire, and the fire storm of passion it created in turn.

"Don't walk away, Rebecca. Not from me, and not from your son."

He lowered his head and his mouth connected with hers. It started out as a simple kiss, just the sweet steady pressure of his lips against hers. But that was all it took for her to recall the predatory claim of his hands, the gentle possession of his lips and tongue. Her lips parted and she sighed as he deepened the kiss with masterful strokes of his tongue. She was surrounded with the warm male scent of him, seduced by the strength of his arms around her. Heat pooled between her thighs. Her body melted in surrender and it was all she could do not to succumb, not to make love to him then and there, but the thought of her grandparents just upstairs soon put a damper on her ardor.

She pushed away from him, chest heaving. "I have to go, Jack."

He gave her a sexy grin, as if he thought he was winning this battle of wills. "For now?" he asked with a shameless grin.

Rebecca blushed all the hotter despite her decision not to. "Yes."

"Why?" He drew back just enough to give her room to breathe, not enough room to escape.

She leaned as far back into the counter, as far back away from him as she could. "Because when you kiss me like that I can't think straight," she admitted on a tremulous sigh.

He braced a hand on either side of her. "And that's bad?"

"When I lose sight of reality, it is."

Jack met her level gaze affably and gave her another coaxing grin. "The reality is that you, me and Andy could all be together as a family one day."

Her heart aching, Rebecca traced a line down the middle of his chest with her fingertip. She wanted to believe that. But the cold hard facts of the situation kept reminding her otherwise. "Is it? You wouldn't even be here, Jack, if that baby hadn't been left on Alec Roman's doorstep. You never would have even seen me again."

Jack straightened. "Don't be so sure of that."

Rebecca lifted her head in surprise. "You had plans to come and see me again?"

He frowned and didn't reply.

"Just as I thought!" Rebecca lifted a braced arm and stormed off.

He caught up with her just as she reached the living room. Circling around her, he cut off her path to the stairs and the safety of the second floor. "What does it matter how things were? We're together again now."

"But for how long, Jack?" Rebecca shot back as she propped both her hands on her hips. "How long before you realize this baby really doesn't belong with us, but to someone else?"

"You mean that, don't you?" Jack asked slowly.

Rebecca nodded. Her heart constricted painfully in her chest. "I didn't believe you at first, either. I thought that you were just here because you guessed I was Andy's mother. Then, I thought you stayed because you had decided I'd be a good mother, anyway, even if I wasn't the biological mother. But now I've been around you enough to believe you when you tell me there was no other woman in your life at the time we met...and if that's the case, then Andy really doesn't belong to either of us! And if that's the case, Jack, someone is missing an adorable two-month-old baby. And if that's true, then you better go back to Philadelphia and try to find Andy's real parents!"

"I'M GETTING TO BE an old pro at this. Know that, kiddo?" Jack asked as he lifted Andy out of the shallow basin that was serving as bathtub and wrapped him in a towel.

Andy stared up at Jack, his blue eyes happy and alert, as Jack carried Andy over to the double bed. He had everything laid out—baby powder, nighttime diaper, clean undershirt and blanket sleeper. "I bet I could even dress you in the dark with both hands tied behind my back," Jack teased.

Andy gurgled in response and tried to bat his way out of the towel Jack had wrapped him in.

Jack grinned and freed his son from the towel. "Okay," he allowed, "make that in a dimly lit room with one hand tied behind my back." He slid the diaper beneath him and then powdered Andy's bottom. "The two of us have bonded faster than I ever imagined we could. You and I are family, Andy. Family."

But what if they weren't? Jack thought uncomfortably as he fastened Andy's diaper and reached for his T-shirt.

The note left with Andy hadn't named a specific name. It had just said, "To Andy's father." Andy had been left on Alec Roman's doorstep, not Jack's. Most damning of all, Jack knew what Rebecca did not. That Alec had already mistakenly claimed Andy as *his* child for almost an entire week before Alec had figured out that Andy wasn't Alec's baby at all...and called Jack. The two of them had quickly consulted their calendars and decided Andy was Jack's baby. Jack had hopped the first flight to Philly, picked up Andy and tracked down Rebecca in short order.

But now everything was falling apart, Jack mused silently as he slid first one of Andy's wildly waving arms into the T-shirt, and then the other, then snapped it in the front.

Jack smiled at his son and chucked him under his cute chin. "Rebecca adores you, sport, I know that," he said softly as he reached for Andy's thick, soft blanket sleeper. "But the more I'm around her, the more I think that maybe, just maybe, she might be telling me the truth about your not being her baby after all. And that scares me," Jack admitted as he zipped Andy into the nighttime sleeper.

Andy's expression turned as glum as Jack's. He kicked Jack on the thigh, once and then again, demanding silently, it seemed, to be picked up.

Deciding some prebedtime cuddling was in order, Jack picked Andy up, and then scooted back on the bed until he was propped up against the headboard. "This better?" Jack asked as he turned his son onto his tummy and then placed Andy on his chest. Andy banged a fist on Jack's chest and made a sound that indicated agreement. It would be a few minutes before Andy was ready to go to sleep. He liked to be talked to or sung to in the interim. Jack figured he might as well continue his verbal theorizing.

"Okay, so where were we?" Jack asked Andy. Remembering, Jack sighed, "Oh, yeah, we were talking about whether or not we should believe her when she says you're not her baby."

Andy gurgled and frowned, then looked at Jack as if he wanted Jack to go on with the story.

"As I said, part of me does want to believe her. After all, how could I care about a woman who lied to me about something as important as this? And I do care about Rebecca, Andy, very much. Besides, just look at the facts. Rebecca is headstrong, and impulsive, but she wouldn't leave you on a doorstep and walk off and leave you with a complete stranger, would she?" Jack asked.

Andy pushed himself up, thumped his fist on Jack's chest, then shook his head restlessly from side to side.

Jack grinned at Andy's seeming rejection of that theory. "My thoughts exactly, buddy," Jack said. "On the other hand, whoever did leave you on Alec's doorstep on Valentine's Day did wait until Alec got home before he or she put your bassinet on the front stoop and rang the bell. Whoever left you cared what happened to you. And we know that Alec's house was the only place where Rebecca knew to reach me... so she could have done it."

Jack fell silent a moment. Tiring, Andy dropped his head back to Jack's chest and cuddled against him. Jack continued to gently stroke Andy's back with tender, sleep-inducing motions.

"And," Jack continued softly, "we also know that Rebecca went off to Indiana for six months and that just before she left, she was very upset, withdrawn and physically ill...so ill that Ruth and Eli insisted she see the doctor. All that, my good buddy, points to a pregnancy."

Jack looked down at Andy and saw his son was fast asleep. He was reluctant to let him go. Jack had yet to get over the wonder of holding a baby close, of feeling the love and tenderness that poured out of him whenever he was around Andy.

"The last few days have changed me, Andy," he said softly. Just like the week that Andy had spent with Alec had changed Alec. Fatherhood had brought a dimension of happiness to Jack's life that he hadn't known was possible. And Jack didn't want to give that happiness, or Rebecca, up. And yet, if Rebecca was telling the truth about Andy truly not belonging to her...

Jack held Andy close and breathed in the baby-fresh scent of his skin and hair. How could Andy not be his and Rebecca's child? he wondered desperately. Andy had big blue eyes, and fair, flawless skin, just like Rebecca's. He had curly dark hair, just like Jack's mom. Or did he?

Maybe what he saw as proof was nothing more than coincidence, no matter how much he wanted to believe otherwise. There was no other reason Rebecca would tell Jack that the baby wasn't hers, or suggest not so subtly that Jack needed to be away from Blair County and out looking for Andy's real parents, unless...

Jack winced as the next idea struck.

No. It couldn't be...could it? She wouldn't do that to him. *Would she?*

"I THOUGHT YOU WOULD have been packing to leave by now," Rebecca said first thing the next morning when she encountered Jack in the kitchen, heating Andy's bottle.

"I just bet you did," Jack drawled agreeably. "Unfortunately for you, Rebecca, I am not in the mood to go off hunting any wild moose."

Rebecca flushed in a way that made Jack sure she was guilty. "What are you talking about now, Jack?"

Jack leaned closer and whispered in her ear, "I'm talking about the way you successfully got rid of Levi and Dieter when they were pestering you unbearably. You laid some false tracks in the woods and then sent them off on a wild moose chase. Only I'm not falling for it, Rebecca, and neither is Andy."

Rebecca's blue eyes widened with amazement. "Is that what you think I did?" she asked dryly.

Jack shrugged, not about to let Rebecca throw him off with another display of innocence. "It's the only explanation that fits, when you and I both know Andy is our child.''

Rebecca tossed Jack an exasperated glance. ''You've got everything figured out, haven't you, Jack?''

Jack shifted Andy a little higher in his arms. ''I even know why you were so desperate to have me out of here that you'd do such a low-down thing,'' he confided assuredly.

Rebecca's chin took on a stubborn tilt. She turned away from both Jack and Andy and stirred the kettle of oatmeal cooking on the stove. ''And why is that, Jack?''

Jack watched Rebecca add chopped apples and raisins to the cooking cereal. The long night had given him a chance to come to terms with her actions, and put them into perspective. It had also given him time to decide that he wasn't going to leave here before he'd made Rebecca own up to her mistakes. ''You want to get rid of me,'' Jack whispered in her ear, aware they could conceivably be walked in on at any minute, ''because I've made no secret of the fact that I want to tell your grandparents everything, and you're not willing to do that.''

Rebecca set her spoon down with a thud and turned to face Jack. Her expression was fierce. ''I told you, before, Jack, I do not want to hurt them.''

''What about me?'' Jack asked. ''What about Andy? Don't our feelings count?'' He stroked a hand through Andy's dark curly hair.

Rebecca reached up to gently stroke Andy's downy soft cheek. "I don't want this baby hurt, either," she whispered, really seeming to mean it.

Jack sighed and took another step closer to her. "Then why don't you stop using all your energy to push the two of us away," he asked softly, "and instead, start concentrating on overcoming the logistical problems of merging our two very diverse lives? Because once you do that, Rebecca," Jack murmured encouragingly, the three of us will finally be able to become the family we were meant to be."

"WE'RE GOING TO NEED more tea and more sugar for the frolic today," Ruth said, several hours later.

Jack looked up from the notes he had been making on Amish homes. "Do you want me to stop in town and get supplies before I drive out to the Yoders?" He owed the Lindholm family a lot. They had not only been gracious hosts, but extremely generous in sharing their knowledge of Amish ways.

"That would be a help to us," Eli said, "as I would like to be one of the first to arrive at the Yoders. The young men need us older men to help get them organized."

"And if you wouldn't mind, Jack, I'd like to take Andy with us," Ruth said.

"She wants to show him off," Eli joked with a teasing glance at his wife. He watched as Ruth bundled Andy up in a snowsuit, cap and blanket. "You're acting as if he's your own grandchild."

"I am not. Well..." Ruth allowed with a blush that was almost girlish in its innocence. "Maybe just a little, but I can't help it. It's been such a long time since we've had a little one in this house to love...you know we never really had you at that age, Rebecca, except for the occasional visit."

"I know."

"I missed watching you grow up."

Rebecca smiled back at her grandparents. "Well, you've got me now."

"That I do. So Jack... the baby?" Ruth asked.

"I'd be honored if you'd take him with you," Jack said. "That way I'll have my arms free to help Rebecca at the store."

"We'll see you at the Yoders then." Eli and Ruth went on, Andy in Ruth's arms.

Jack turned to Rebecca. "Ready to go?"

Rebecca nodded at him curtly. "Just as soon as I get my bonnet."

They went outside together. Jack gave Rebecca a hand up into the buggy. "You going to let me drive today?" he asked as he slid in beside her.

Rebecca gave him a sidelong glance. "Do you want to?"

Jack shrugged. "If I'm going to become Amish, I need to learn basic survival skills."

Rebecca gave him a sharp look as he took up the reins. "I told you not to toy with me, Jack."

"I'm not." Jack paused, then continued softly, "It occurred to me last night that I was asking you to give up everything and offering nothing in return." Jack frowned. "Maybe it's time that changed, Rebecca."

Rebecca regarded him suspiciously. "What does that mean? What are you trying to tell me?"

Still feeling a little unsure of his ability to drive a horse and buggy, Jack tightened his grip on the reins as the buggy headed out into the main road. "If Mohammed won't come to the mountain, then the mountain will go to Mohammed," he said.

Rebecca gaped at him in surprise. "You would do that for me?" she whispered. "Actually move here, and perhaps even become Amish, to be close to me?"

Jack shrugged. "If it's the only way to get you to admit to being Andy's mother and give us a chance, sure, why not?"

Rebecca scowled and folded her arms in front of her. "You're talking nonsense again."

"Yeah, but it's a nonsense we both understand," Jack said. He cast her a sidelong glance. "What are we doing at the Yoders today?"

Rebecca looked relieved at the opportunity to talk about something else. "The widow Yoder needs a new roof, so we're having a frolic—a day of unpaid labor—to help her. Everyone in our community is going to be there."

"It sounds like fun," Jack said.

"It will be," Rebecca promised.

And it was. The men spent the morning tearing off the old roof. By the time they stopped for the noon meal, they had a new layer of plywood subroofing on. They stopped for dinner as the sun rose high overhead, the men eating first at long plank tables that had been set up outside. The food was hot and delicious, the company entertaining, but Jack had eyes only for Rebecca as she moved easily among her friends and neighbors, never quite meeting Jack's eyes, but never quite taking her eyes off him, either.

"YOU'RE SURE YOU WANT to take Andy home with the two of you?" Jack asked Ruth and Eli.

Ruth nodded, looking completely content with a snugly wrapped Andy curled up in her arms. He was sound asleep, and had been for at least half an hour—and no wonder. There hadn't been a moment all day when the women hadn't been fussing over him appreciatively. The way things were going, Andy was going to grow up thinking he was the most adorable baby on this earth. And why not? Jack thought. He was.

"You and Rebecca can stay and visit with the young people a few extra minutes," Ruth told Jack with a smile as she settled back in the covered black buggy. "It'll give you a few minutes to gather more research for your movie."

"Thanks, Ruth." Jack smiled. "I appreciate your thoughtfulness."

Half an hour later, they were finally on their way. "You must be tired," Rebecca said quietly.

Jack slanted her an amused glance. The truth was, he was a little stiff and sore. He wasn't used to standing on a roof for hours on end. But he'd gotten the hang of it quickly enough. Even Eli, one of the toughest taskmasters there, had been proud. "Think

I'm not tough enough to handle a day of roofing?" he drawled.

"Correct me if I'm wrong," she teased back, "but you rarely spend an entire day wielding a hammer."

"True. But I'm not in such bad shape that I can't take a day of hard physical labor. Being sent on a wild moose hunt, now that's another matter," Jack snapped back as he transferred the reins to one hand.

"What I told you last night... about Andy possibly being some other couple's baby... was sincere, Jack."

Seeing the covered bridge up ahead, he stopped their buggy just inside. Jack dropped the reins and turned toward her. "Sure you weren't just trying to get rid of me because I've been so pesky lately?"

"I admit I've thought about it, but no, I haven't."

"Right," Jack quipped, as he took her all the way into his arms and kissed her thoroughly. She resisted at first. He didn't care. He wasn't letting her shy away from their feelings this time. After a moment, the only sounds in their buggy were the ragged gasp of their breaths, the soft sighs, the rustle of clothing. When he released her at long last, they were both trembling.

"I want you, Rebecca," he said softly, lifting her chin. "I want you so much it hurts. Not just physically, but in my life. In my home."

For a moment, she looked like she wanted to say something to him, too. What exactly, he didn't know. But the moment passed and she turned her eyes from him. He was about to take her into his arms again and kiss her senseless one more time when the sound of another buggy approaching behind them made him pick up the reins and reluctantly resume their journey.

Rebecca peered around the edge of the buggy. She hugged her arms close to her chest. "You shouldn't have done that," she said. "It isn't even dark yet. Someone could have seen us."

"I don't want your reputation in the community hurt on my account, but as for the rest of it, Rebecca, I don't care who knows we have a lot to work out."

"About the baby," Rebecca said, her expression going from wistful to deeply troubled in a matter of seconds.

"And us," Jack confirmed. "I know we began our relationship the opposite way we should have. But we can't go back and change that, Rebecca. All we can do is start again."

Rebecca paused, her expression uncertain. "The baby aside . . . you really think we could do that?"

"I know we could," Jack said firmly. Around them, darkness continued to fall, and they passed other buggies on the road. "Especially now that I've met your family. Ruth and Eli like me. And they love Andy as they would their own grandchild."

Rebecca's mouth tightened. "I don't want to be some Amish trophy you've collected in your travels, Jack."

"I never said you would."

"But you are fascinated—at least for the moment—with our quaint Amish ways. And don't try and deny it."

"I admit I am fascinated by the self-sufficiency of the Amish, the sense of community, the way you take care of your old people and one another. But that's not all it is."

"I know," she said in a flip tone of voice. "With me, it's sex."

"Making love," Jack corrected, his own temper heating up at Rebecca's continued obstinacy, her refusal to even give them a chance to live as a couple, as a family, with their son. He slanted her a deliberately rapacious glance. "And that's not so bad, either, judging from your passionate response the one night you spent in my bed. Or were you making up those little moans you made when I—"

"I told you I did not want to discuss that!"

Jack watched Rebecca flush a bright pink. So she hadn't forgotten her response to him, he thought victoriously. "Don't expect me to ever let you forget it. Particularly," he added forcefully when she was about to interrupt, "since your family is no longer standing in the way of us. Not in any real sense."

"My family does not make my decisions. I do." There was no confusion in her light blue eyes as she looked at him. Sensual awareness, yes. Wavering of opinion, no.

"And I think you're a bad risk," Rebecca continued stubbornly, her soft pink mouth taking on a determined pout. "One I have absolutely no intention of taking. You're wasting your time here, Jack. When are you going to get that through your thick head?"

Chapter Eight

"Jack did well at the frolic today," Ruth said as the two women washed the dishes a scant hour and a half later. The men were outside, tending to the animals. Baby Andy was in his infant seat, his rattle clutched tightly in his hand as he followed the two women around the room with his eyes.

"Yes, he did," Rebecca said, and unable to help herself, she screwed up her nose at baby Andy, who broke into a wide grin. Gurgling at her, he enthusiastically waved his rattle around in front of his cherubic face.

Ruth patted Andy's sleeper-covered foot. "Little Andy needs a mother to love him. It's a shame Jack is not Amish. If he were, there would be plenty of women around to love and nurture Andy. I am afraid that is not the case in California."

Rebecca dried the last dish and put it away while her grandmother began wiping the counters. "I'm sure Jack will find someone to take good care of little Andy while he works."

Hearing her voice, Andy grinned at her again. He waved his rattle excitedly, and bumped himself in the nose. At the contact of blue plastic against his face, he let out a startled cry. Rebecca scooped him up in her arms and held him close. "There, there now," she soothed, breathing in the fresh baby scent of him. A wave of contentment swept through Rebecca. Sometimes she thought this was what life was all about.

Watching, her grandmother looked sad. "It's hard for you, isn't it?" she said softly. "Not having a child of your own."

"Maybe I will someday," Rebecca said, pushing the longing she felt away.

The truth of the matter was she could have Andy now, if she really wanted him. All she had to do was claim him as her own. Jack would marry her. Instant family. She even sensed, if she absolutely insisted, that she might be able to get Jack to stay in the area, perhaps even become Amish himself. At least for a while. But she also knew that he would eventually tire of their quaint ways. He was no different than the tourists who flocked to see the Pennsylvania Amish every summer. And sooner or later, the truth would come out about the baby, too. She couldn't live a lie, any more than she could live as the principal player of some romantic fantasy on Jack's part.

"Are you and Jack going to go skating on the Danhof's place tonight?" Ruth asked.

Rebecca shrugged and shifted the baby to her other shoulder. "I haven't asked him," she admitted. And for good reason. Aware her grandmother was watching her thoughtfully, Rebecca continued, "I don't even know if he knows how to ice skate."

"Sure I know how to ice skate," Jack said as he and Eli trooped in to join them. He warmed his hands next to the stove. "I grew up in Pennsylvania, remember?"

"Still, it's been an awfully long day," Rebecca said.

His eyes met and held hers. He bent and kissed his son on the cheek. "It sounds like fun."

"It will be," Ruth said. "All the young people will be there."

Jack cast another look at Rebecca, and his expression gentled even more. She realized she still had the baby in her arms. He was looking at the two of them as if they belonged together, not as temporary caretaker and child, but as mother and son. She felt herself flush. She knew she was holding Andy tenderly, and with great joy, but she knew no other way to hold him.

Jack's glance cut back to Ruth. "You're sure you don't mind watching Andy?"

"Not at all," Ruth said. She held out her arms to Andy, who went to her happily.

Jack turned to Rebecca. "Do you have any skates I could borrow?"

"You can take mine," Eli said.

"Thank you. That's very kind of you," Jack said. He turned to Rebecca. "Let's go."

"I WASN'T KIDDING earlier," Jack said as the two of them strolled side by side down the path that led to the

Danhof's pond. Because it was right next door to the Lindholm farm, they had elected to walk. "I'm seriously thinking about giving up my home in Los Angeles and moving to Pennsylvania. And I'll do it, too, if it's the only way I can have you."

His words caught her by surprise. She didn't like being pushed into anything. Jack's determination left her feeling a little trapped. "Do you always have to have what you want?" Rebecca asked lightly. She picked up her pace, so she was walking slightly ahead of him.

"In this case, yes." Jack caught up with her, dropped his skates into the snow and took her into his arms. Before she could move to extricate herself, he had clamped an arm around her waist. Her thighs tensed as they nudged his. Lower still, she could feel his arousal as her pulse pounded in her throat, and her hunger for him inundated her with tidal-wave force. Her fingers tightened on the knotted shoestring that connected her skates.

"Being with you again has made me realize what I think I knew in my heart all along," Jack confided in a low, compelling voice.

Wordlessly he wrested her skates from her hands and dropped them beside his. It was a simple action. Innocent almost. And yet nearly as sexy as undressing in front of him had been.

Rebecca could hear the jerky sound of her breathing, feel the traitorous tensing of her body as his thumb traced the line of her jaw, then moved up to brush across her lower lip. His smile softened tenderly. "You and I are destined to be together, Rebecca," he confided hoarsely, his eyes darkening to a deep Aegean blue, "we have been from the very first."

Rebecca had expected him to put the moves on her again, but not this soon. She knew she shouldn't let him kiss her again, but even as his head was lowering, her eyes were closing and her lips were parting. She drifted toward him, against him, aching with need, awash with anticipation. The first touch of his mouth against hers flooded her with dizzying waves of desire. Rebecca had never felt anything like what she felt with Jack. Never wanted this way. Never needed. Never even dreamed feeling this way was possible.

Unable to stop herself, she moaned low in her throat and went more fully into his arms, lacing her hands around his shoulders and pressing her body close to his, until they touched from breastbone to knee in one unbroken line. And still they kissed, until she was weak with wanting him, weak with need. Until he was all she could think of, all she could feel....

Slowly he drew away. Rebecca looked up at him, her gaze misty and bewildered. "I don't need an answer now," Jack told her softly, gazing down at her and caressing the side of her face with the back of his hand. He had never felt skin so silky soft. "I just want you to think about it, Rebecca, to know the possibility of my moving here to be with you exists."

As what? she wondered. His mistress? As a live-in nanny for his son? Because that was all he seemed to be offering her. Steadying a bit, she forced herself to step out of his arms. Wordlessly she picked up her skates and handed him his.

"You're awfully quiet." Jack cast her an interested sidelong glance. Moonlight filtered down through the trees, as bright as any electric porch light.

That's because I'm trying not to fall in love with you, Rebecca thought as she tightened her gloved hands into fists to stop their trembling. "We're going to be late for the skating party, Jack," she said, deliberately sidestepping any more attempts at intimate conversation. "We had better hurry." Not waiting for him to reply, for fear if she did he would use the opportunity to kiss her again, she turned and hurried down the path, all too aware he was just half a step behind her.

Unfortunately they were the last to arrive at the Danhof's farm. As Rebecca had predicted, her tardiness was noted by all. "Hey Rebecca," Levi said, crossing to her side immediately. He was wearing a forbidden bright red sweatshirt beneath his black Amish coat. "What took you so long?"

"I wanted to help my grandmother with the dishes before I left." Rebecca sat down on a log before the pond's edge to put on her skates. Times like this, when she was forced to be outdoors in the winter in a dress and black wool stockings, instead of warm wool slacks, she resented some of the restrictions of Amish life. But she supposed that came from all the time she had spent early on, and then again later, living English.

''Sure that's all that was keeping you?'' Dieter sat down on the other side of her and Jack. Like Levi, he was wearing a forbidden item of clothing as an open sign of his youthful rebelliousness. In his case, it was a bright orange-and-black knit Cincinnati Bengals cap. He wrapped a teasing arm around her shoulders and looked into her face. ''Your cheeks are a little pink.''

''You know what I think?'' Rebecca shot back, ignoring the way Jack was glaring at Dieter and the possessive arm Dieter had laced around her shoulders. ''I think all the skating you have done tonight has addled your brains, Dieter.'' Rebecca tugged the laces of her skates tight.

''Maybe, but then I'm not the one head over heels in love with you,'' Dieter remarked. He stood and pulled some wintergreen breath mints out of his pants pocket. ''My cousin Levi is.''

Laughter erupted from the group quickly gathering around them. Levi gave Dieter a teasing poke in the ribs. Dieter poked back. The next thing Rebecca knew the two teenage boys were wrestling around on the snowy ground. Lifting her glance heavenward and shaking her head in silent remonstration, she headed for the ice.

Jack was fast on her heels. To her dismay, she found he was an excellent ice skater. No matter how swiftly she skated, he kept pace with her, easily overtaking her with his long smooth glides. ''The teasing upset you.'' Hands behind him, he skated around her in a lazy figure eight.

Rebecca shrugged as at the other end of the ice, Dieter and Levi picked up a pair of hockey sticks and a round plastic disk. "Dieter and Levi are always clowning around."

"They're also both in love with you."

Rebecca inclined her head slightly to the side. "Not according to Dieter."

"You know what they say about boys that age. Their actions paint a truer picture than their words, and those two are devoted to you."

Rebecca couldn't argue that. Since she had returned to Pennsylvania after her divorce, those two boys had appointed themselves her honorary kid brothers. And like all kid brothers, they could be bratty and rude and fiercely protective. Right now, they still hadn't figured out if Jack was friend or foe; all they knew for sure was that he had an unusually strong effect on Rebecca. She shrugged again. "They have girls they are courting."

"But only because you won't give them the chance."

Rebecca grinned at Jack. There was no reason for him to feel jealous. But she was kind of enjoying seeing him act that way, anyway. "They're too young for me."

"I agree." Jack laced his hand through her elbow, then pushed her forward with his other hand, just in time to avoid a flying hockey puck. "You need someone a few years older than yourself, like me."

Rebecca extricated her arm from his and skated forward. It was a cold night, but she felt warm all over. "Stop it," she said in a low voice.

"Stop what?" He gave her a look of comically exaggerated innocence.

"Courting me so obviously!" Rebecca hissed back, as the flush that had been rising in her neck travelled to her cheeks as well.

Jack matched his glides to hers. Half his mouth crooked up in a rueful grin as he put his hands behind him again. "Why?"

Rebecca did a swift about-face that made her skates cut a swath in the ice. Almost beside herself with the attention they were earning, she put her hands on her hips. "Because I've never been very good at hiding my feelings!" she blurted out in exasperation, before she could think. Jack's grin widened mischievously. "That's what got me into trouble with you in the first place," she said sternly, regarding him with a challenging glare. "One look into my eyes, and you know exactly what I'm thinking and feeling."

"Not always," he disagreed, wishing he could take her hand in his the way he had in the woods. But that would cause a scandal. Even linking his arm through hers had been over the line....

"I am going over to talk to the other girls," Rebecca said, doing another fast about-face and skating off. Jack was about to follow her, when Dieter and Levi skated up to him. One on either side of him, they more or less commanded him to the pond's edge, and the picnic table of refreshments that had been set up there. "We want to talk to you," Dieter said.

Big surprise there, Jack thought as he helped himself to a cup of hot chocolate from the gallon thermos. Steam rose from the cup as he lifted it to his mouth. "What about?" he asked.

"We don't want to see Rebecca get hurt," Levi said.

"Ja," Dieter agreed, "she was hurt enough by her first marriage to that other Englishman."

Jack tore his eyes from Rebecca and the group of young women she was standing with. *Rebecca had been married to another Englishman?*

"Ja," Levi continued. He tapped his index finger against Jack's breastbone in a threatening manner. "We don't want any other Englishman marrying her and then dumping and divorcing her like yesterday's outgrown clothing."

Jack stared at them in shock. "Rebecca was married to an Englishman?" he asked, irritated to be hearing it from them, and not her. And for that matter, *why* hadn't she told him this?

"When she was in Florida," Dieter affirmed.

Levi stared at Jack suspiciously. "You're telling us you didn't know?" he said.

"That's putting it lightly," Jack said through his teeth. Once again, everything he had thought about Rebecca was a lie. She wasn't a widow. She was divorced. She hadn't married a nice Amish boy from around there, as her grandparents obviously would have preferred, but an English man, in Florida. His temper spinning out of control, he wondered what else he didn't know.

JACK WAS ODDLY SILENT as they started home. Rebecca didn't know what Levi and Dieter had said to Jack when they'd been drinking hot chocolate, but whatever it was had upset him.

"You must be exhausted," Rebecca murmured as she and Jack walked through the woods that separated the Danhof property from the Lindholm farm. In the past hour, a winter storm front had begun to move in. The stars were no longer visible and the sky had grown cloudy. Tiny flakes of snow had begun to fall. The woods were hushed and quiet. "First the frolic, then the evening chores," Rebecca recited casually, not wanting to admit how Jack's continued silence and brooding looks were unnerving her. She drew a shallow breath. "Ice skating after that."

"It's not fatigue that's bothering me," Jack said shortly. His mouth tightened even more.

Rebecca shivered in a way that had little to do with the cold night air, and dug her hands even deeper into the pockets of her cloak. "Then what is it?"

Jack turned and gave her a measuring look. "The deliberate deceptions."

Rebecca's heart stopped, then resumed a tense jerky rhythm. She forced herself to keep walking, to look straight ahead. She estimated they had another half mile or so to go before they reached the edge of the woods. "What do you mean?"

"I mean . . ." Jack suddenly took her by the shoulder and backed her up against a tree. He braced a hand on either side of her, effectively pinning her in place, and for the second time that night, he tossed both their skates aside. "Why didn't you tell me your first husband was an Englishman? Why didn't you tell me you were divorced? Why did you let me think you were a widow?"

Rebecca swallowed hard. She had never seen him look so angry. Pretending a calmness of spirit she couldn't begin to feel, she kept her hands in her pockets and stared up at him. "I never said I was a widow. You just assumed, Jack."

He clamped the edges of his teeth together. "But you didn't bother to correct me."

It was all Rebecca could do to hold his gaze. Telling herself that she owed Jack nothing—this was her private life after all—she tipped her head back even further. "I didn't think my marital status was any of your business when we first met, so no, I didn't correct you then." She had expected him to be annoyed if and when he found out the truth about her marriage; she hadn't expected this blazing mistrust and resentment. "Besides, you were bound and determined to think what you wanted to about me anyway," she said with a shrug.

Jack dropped his arms and stepped back. "What the hell gave you that idea?" he demanded.

Rebecca straightened against the tree trunk. She propped her hands on her waist and faced him contentiously. "Because I saw the way you looked at me."

He leaned closer, until she had no choice but to inhale the spicy scent of his cologne. "And how, pray tell, was that?" he asked ever so softly.

Rebecca's pulse jumped. Her thighs went a little more fluid. But she held his gaze with all the guts of a prize fighter stepping into the ring. "The same way every Englishman looks when he sees a pretty Amish girl," she said. "You romanticize me. You look at my clothes and assume I'm a pure angel straight out of another time. Well, I'm not. I'm human. I have flaws and faults, just like everyone else. I—make mistakes."

Without warning, Jack's face changed. He girded his thighs and folded his arms in front of him. "Like giving away your only child because you didn't want to face the scandal that trying to raise a baby on your own would cause?"

"I didn't—"

"I know you didn't mean to hurt me." His voice gentled unexpectedly. "And it means a lot that you didn't try to take my child from me, but rather gave him back to me to raise. But—"

"Jack—" Rebecca said wearily.

"You're more selfless than you think, Rebecca."

She shook her head in both bewilderment and chagrin and studied the toe of her sturdy black shoes. If she were selfless, she wouldn't be allowing him to still entertain these fantasies that the baby he'd found was their baby. She'd be working harder to convince him he was wrong about that, and that he had to leave.

That he had to go off and find the baby's real mother. But she wasn't. And why?

The simple truth of the matter was she didn't want Jack to leave. She wanted him to stay right there, pursuing her for all he was worth. She wanted to see where all this lunacy on his part would lead. If he really would relocate to Pennsylvania and try to live Amish, even for a time. And that was wrong of her.

She shook her head glumly in silent self-recrimination. "Right now, I don't feel selfless, Jack. I have no reason to feel that way."

To her surprise, he didn't argue with her, but rather picked up their skates and, taking her hand in his, continued down the path. "Tell me about your divorce."

"Why?" Rebecca tried not to think about how good it felt to hold his hand this way.

Jack was quiet for about ten paces. "Because I think what happened in your marriage has directly affected your feelings about having a relationship with me now," he said softly.

"You're right about that," she said sadly.

"So tell me what happened. How did you end up marrying an Englishman to begin with?" he asked gently, tightening his grip on her hand.

"I was seventeen. I was asked to join the church, but I wasn't really sure whether I wanted to do that or not. Part of me longed for my old life, the life I'd had with my parents. My grandparents understood my need to decide for myself how I wanted to live my life, and they also knew I needed some time apart from them in which to make the decision, so they arranged for me to go to Florida and work at a bed-and-breakfast inn that hired a lot of Amish as contract workers during the winter months, when there's not a lot to do on the farm.'' Rebecca paused. This part was not so easy to explain. ''Soon after I arrived, I caught the eye of the wealthy charming son of the owners.''

''And he seduced you,'' Jack interrupted.

''No.'' Rebecca fiddled with the knotted string tying her skates together. ''He didn't seduce me. He did pursue me in a hot and heavy way, though, and I'm ashamed to say I got caught up in it.'' Her mouth tightened and she blushed. Knowing there was no graceful way to say it, she decided to just spit it out. ''I confused a lusty romance with love, and I eloped with him.''

Again, Jack was silent, taking the information in. ''Then what happened?'' he asked as their footsteps continued to crunch along on the snow and ice-encrusted path.

''We crash-landed into normal life,'' Rebecca replied dryly. ''He went back to law school in Miami, and I moved in with him. And that's when everything began to fall apart.'' Pain laced her heart as she remembered. Rebecca shook her head. ''I just couldn't please him. It wasn't that hard for me to become English again, but after seven years of living with my grandparents, I wasn't quite your everyday new bride, either. To make things worse—'' Rebecca's lip curled bitterly ''—without my Amish ways, I wasn't the pure young innocent maiden Wes had married. And now my Amishness was an embarrassment to him."

"The marriage fell apart in a few months, despite my best efforts to hold things together for both our sakes. It was quite frankly a disaster and I do mean a disaster, and so when Wesley told me he wanted a divorce, I didn't argue with him. I just returned home to my grandparents. I talked to the community about what I had done—"

"Or in other words, you confessed your sins," Jack said.

"Right." Rebecca nodded, at peace with the understanding way she had been taken back into the community. "And they accepted me back, almost as if nothing had happened. Ever since—it's been almost six years now—I've lived Amish. And while it's not a perfect life, sometimes far from it, I also know I am safe and loved and unconditionally accepted here. That's something I never felt while I was in Florida." She gritted her teeth together and glared a warning. "I'm not going to make the same mistake again, Jack—marry someone who has idealized me into his fantasy figure of goodness and purity."

Jack didn't comment either way about that. Tightening his grip on her hand, he asked gently, in a low voice laced with understanding, "Why didn't you tell me any of this sooner?"

Rebecca sighed. How could she explain how foolish just remembering that time of her life made her feel, or how scared she was of repeating her mistakes again? "Because I am and have always been a very private person. Besides, there's no point in me rehashing the details of my failed marriage ad nauseam. It's over. And I want it to stay over, especially now that I'm back where I belong." Jack stopped moving abruptly but kept his grip on her hand. Rebecca stopped, too.

"But do you belong here, Rebecca?" Jack asked softly, looking down at her with all the love and affection she had ever wanted him to feel. "Or do you belong with me and with your child?"

Once again, Rebecca was flooded with guilt. She really should have tried harder to make Jack understand that Andy was not her child. Her heart pounding, she regarded Jack cautiously. "What are you trying to say?"

He lifted his shoulders in a careless shrug. "Simply that the way you've behaved is beginning to make sense to me now. You tried marriage to an Englishman once, and it didn't work. Naturally that made you wary of trying it again. Yet single Amish women do not raise children on their own. So you went to Indiana and had the baby there, and then made arrangements to leave the baby with me—through Alec—instead."

Rebecca released a lengthy sigh. Before she could say anything, Jack rushed to reassure her gently, "It's okay, Rebecca. I understand now. I forgive you."

"There's nothing to forgive," Rebecca muttered.

"Says you. I think there's plenty to forgive. For starters, robbing me of the chance to marry you months ago, watch my baby grow inside you and see my child born."

Her frustration with Jack and his powerful imagination mounting, Rebecca shook her head at him. "Jack. Please. For once, listen to me. Andy is not my child."

He frowned impatiently. "I can't believe, after all you've just told me, that you would still deny it!"

And it was then that Rebecca realized it didn't matter what she said. Jack wasn't going to believe her. He already had his mind made up. What was the point of trying? She'd only be wasting her breath, and both their time.

"Fine. You're right, Jack. The baby is mine," Rebecca said sarcastically, moving forward until they stood toe-to-toe. "I confess, you found me out. I did it all to protect myself. I concocted a crazy story about needing money to fix up my broken down car so I could go off and have the baby in secret in Indiana. I left Andy on Alec's doorstep only because I was too lazy to go all the way to Los Angeles and leave him there. Or maybe I just couldn't recall your last name. Who knows what motivates a selfish, lying, cowardly woman like myself?" In a fury, she stomped off, her ice skates swinging from her hand.

Jack caught up with her. Hand on her shoulder, he swung her around to face him. "Rebecca—"

She started to struggle. He pulled her close. "Don't you understand what I'm trying to tell you? It's all right. I'm here and I'm going to take care of you—"

His head lowered. His mouth hovered just above hers.

"Aha!" a low male voice chortled from behind them. "I told you he'd be sparking her in the trees!"

Jack and Rebecca turned to see Dieter and Levi creeping up behind them. They were still a good ten feet away, but it was obvious they'd managed to see plenty.

His mouth thinning, Jack pushed Rebecca behind him and took a step toward the rowdy teenage boys. "You two are going to have to find something else to do," Jack warned. "Because Rebecca and I are *very tired* of being spied on."

As far as Rebecca was concerned, Dieter and Levi had come just in the nick of time. If they hadn't appeared when they did, she might have gotten just as caught up in all Jack's romantic notions as he was.

"Speak for yourself." Rebecca pushed Jack aside and stepped out in front of him. "Hi, guys," she said flirtatiously. "I was wondering when you two ruffians would show up."

Dieter and Levi grinned back at her mischievously. "Hello, Rebecca," they echoed back in a teasing singsong voice.

"Want a lift home?" Dieter asked.

Rebecca grinned. "You two haven't got a buggy with you," she reminded. It wasn't possible to take a buggy through the woods. The path was only wide enough for walking.

"Ah, but we've got something better! Our brute strength!" Dieter replied. He and Levi rushed forward and lifted her up off the ground.

It didn't take Jack long to realize that Rebecca was enjoying herself. He frowned as the two teenagers carried a laughing Rebecca down the path toward the Lindholm farm. Short of chasing after all three of them, there was nothing Jack could do to stop the shenanigans of the boys.

Well, there wasn't any point in that, Jack thought. Rebecca clearly wasn't in a mood to listen to him. Nor did she seem ready to tell him the whole truth about the baby, at least not yet.

The problem was, he mused, picking up her skates as well as his and sauntering slowly down the path, she still didn't believe he cared about *her* at all. He had hoped his mere presence here would prove that was the case. And if not that, his kisses. Obviously it just wasn't enough.

Maybe she needed more tangible proof, he thought. Like a serious proposal and an engagement ring. *Was he ready for that?* Or maybe she just needed to be loved again, as thoroughly as he had loved her the first time.

The question was how could he make that happen. They were never alone very long. And when they were, they generally had the baby with them.

Of course, they'd have to get used to that. Interruptions would probably be par for the course from now on. The trick would be in making the most of the time they had. As for tonight...well, Jack thought as he watched Dieter and Levi put Rebecca down near the Lindholm farmhouse, Levi and Dieter had definitely thwarted his efforts to get close to Rebecca tonight.

Rebecca had gone along with them to prevent any more intimate discussions of what she had done in the past or might do in the future. So she'd been saved this time. Temporarily. But she wouldn't be saved the next, Jack vowed. Because one way or another, they were going to work this out. He was going to get close to her again. And from there, who only knew what would happen?

Chapter Nine

"I knew you wouldn't be able to stay away from him indefinitely," Jack said just before noon the next day.

Rebecca whirled away from the cradle. Her cheeks were pink with embarrassment, even as the soft sound of her singing and Andy's delighted gurgles echoed in the room. "I was just singing Andy a lullaby," she said defensively. "I didn't think you'd mind."

Jack closed the distance between them and wrapped an arm around her waist. "Of course I don't mind," he said, loving the way she felt against him, so soft and warm and womanly. He bent his head lower and breathed in the silky floral essence of her hair. "I want you to be close to our son."

"Jack!" Rebecca chided, twisting away from his seeking mouth.

Jack put a hold on the kisses, but he didn't let her go. "There's no one here but us," he said. Unfortunately he hadn't been able to take advantage of that fact until now because he'd been away most of the morning, too, checking out a "modern Amish" dairy operation, two farms up the road.

"My grandparents will be back from town at any moment." Rebecca drew herself straight and eased from his arms.

Jack let her go reluctantly, then followed her to the stove, where dinner was cooking. As always, she was wearing a freshly starched and ironed blue cotton knit dress and black cotton apron. And though there was nothing impure about her clothes, there was plenty impure with the way she looked at him whenever she thought he wasn't looking and/or no one else could see.

"Admit it, Rebecca," he coaxed softly. With the tip of his finger, he traced one of the white organdy kapp strings that fell onto her shoulders. "As much as you try to keep your distance, you can't help but love our baby."

Rebecca turned and gave him a brisk smile. She went back to the table, where she had laid out all sizes of fabric in a mesmerizing, clever and eye-catching patchwork design. Scattered across the living room were stacks of other patches in all sorts of colors, layers of soft white cotton that would serve as the middle layer of the quilts. "Your imagination is working overtime again. And I really don't have time for it this morning. We're having a quilting bee here this afternoon. The ladies will start arriving by one."

Jack frowned. Just what he needed. Another day with very little chance to be alone with Rebecca. Soon the nonfiction article he had been commissioned to write to promote the movie would be finished. He couldn't stay away from the set forever. As screenwriter, it was his job to be available for any rewrites that came up during the filming. "How many ladies?"

"Anywhere from ten to twenty, and their children, depending on who shows up," she said. She paused. "Would you mind going upstairs and bringing down the wicker basket that contains all my thread?"

"Not at all," Jack said, "provided you first talk to me about your feelings about our baby."

Rebecca stiffened. "There's no special love in my heart for baby Andy, Jack."

"If I believe that, I would have left days ago. Besides." Jack pulled a chair out, turned it around backward and sat down next to the table. "I saw the way you looked at him just now."

Rebecca glanced up from her work. "To me, Jack, all children are special."

"I don't understand why you won't admit he's yours, then," Jack said, not bothering to hide his frustration with her and her secrets. "Dammit, Rebecca, I've come back for you. Doesn't that count for anything?" he demanded gruffly.

Before Rebecca could reply to that, the sound of the horse and buggy outside had her rushing to the window. "My grandparents are back."

Seconds later, Eli and Ruth came in, carrying two bolts of fabric and a can of kerosene for the lamps. To Jack's surprise, their expressions were grim. "What is it?" Rebecca asked immediately.

Eli removed his black hat and took off his heavy wool overcoat. He motioned for Rebecca to sit. "I don't want to upset you, Rebecca, but there was some talk in town. Dieter and Levi said they interrupted a...well, a private moment between the two of you in the woods last night. Is this true?''

For a second, the silence in the room was so intense you could have heard a pin drop. ''Jack and I were talking,'' Rebecca admitted. She sat straighter and put both her hands in her lap.

''They made it sound like more than that,'' Ruth said, her expression worried as she sat down at the table beside Rebecca.

Eli's frown deepened. ''Someone else said they saw the two of you parked in a buggy inside a covered bridge before the frolic at the Yoders yesterday.''

Jack felt a pang of guilt. He wondered if they had also seen him kiss Rebecca. Rebecca got up and went to the stove. She stirred the stew. ''I've been teaching Jack to drive the buggy,'' Rebecca said as she put the wooden spoon back on the ceramic spoon rest.

''Unfortunately,'' Jack cut in protectively, ''I'm not very good at it. Yet, anyway.'' He was determined to do what he could to protect Rebecca.

''So there's nothing between the two of you?'' Ruth asked.

''No,'' Rebecca said swiftly and she looked straight at Jack. ''Nor could there ever be.''

Her words were quiet and almost expressionless, but Jack felt them like an arrow to the heart. He looked back at her. Now was the time to level with her grandparents. Or was it? What if he told them how he felt about their granddaughter and they asked him to leave? What then? If he no longer had the Lindholm family's support in the community, he wouldn't even be able to see her.

"You still need to be careful," Eli warned Rebecca. He poured himself a cup of coffee from the pot simmering on the back of the stove. "You know how talk can spread, Rebecca."

She nodded, chastened. Her face was pale. "I'm sorry if any of this upset you," Jack said to Ruth and Eli. He looked them both in the eye. "I never wanted to bring any harm to your family."

"I know that," Ruth said. Beside her, Eli remained ominously quiet. Rebecca checked the whole-wheat bread baking inside the oven. Again, silence fell over them like a funeral pall.

For the first time, Jack realized what a scandal an illegitimate pregnancy would cause in the community, particularly if the unwed mother were Rebecca, and he the father. People had seen the two of them in a compromising position, not even kissing, and already the community was buzzing with talk about the two of them. Rebecca's past marriage to another Englishman made things all the worse.

The sound of a car outside interrupted Jack's thoughts. He moved to the window and saw a Federal Express delivery van parked outside. He swore silently to himself. He needed this like he needed a hole in the head. "It's probably for me," Jack said with a sinking heart as he stepped outside. He had told the studio where he could be reached, but he hadn't wanted them to contact him here.

"What is it?" Rebecca asked, long moments later, after Jack had taken the package inside and studied the pages inside thoroughly. He spoke without looking up. The stress of the moment forgotten, his mind was all on his work. "It's the studio. They've decided they need another scene written immediately. What they want isn't all that difficult, but it's going to require a lot of concentration." He looked up, his mind already speeding ahead, estimating the number of hours he thought it would take to complete the scene. Eight, he figured. Ten, at the very most. It would depend on how many interruptions he had. "Can I use your phone?"

The Lindholms grinned in unison. "We have no phone," Rebecca reminded him patiently.

It was all Jack could do to stifle a groan.

He looked at the new quilt she was piecing together on the kitchen table, then down at the pages in his hand. "I'll have to go in to town and make the call from there, then," he said, irritated to have to leave Rebecca again, when he'd already been gone all morning, but there was no helping it. He crossed to the cradle, then saw Andy had just fallen asleep.

"We'll watch the baby," Ruth said. "That way you won't have to wake him."

"Thanks," Jack said. "Andy gets really cranky when he doesn't get to finish his nap."

"Does this work you received mean you're going to have to go back to California sooner than you thought?" Eli asked Jack.

Her face white, Rebecca turned away. But not before Jack had picked up on the raw disappointment in her eyes. Rebecca doesn't want me to leave, either, he thought. His spirits lifting at that small sign of encouragement from her, he turned back to Eli and said, "I hope not." A trip to California now would undercut everything he had accomplished. "But right now it's too soon to tell."

"I PROMISE I'LL HAVE the new scene faxed to you by 9:00 a.m. tomorrow morning," Jack said, struggling to be heard above the clatter of buggies and automobiles in the streets.

"Jack, we need you here," the director said.

"I'm wrapping things up out here as quickly as I can," Jack said, irritated his fantasies of sweeping Rebecca off her feet hadn't begun to come true. She might still desire him, but she wasn't about to marry him, never mind admit the two of them had a baby together.

"By the end of the week," the director stipulated firmly, "or I'm hiring another writer to finish the film for you."

That didn't give him much time, Jack thought, frowning. He was going to have to work faster than he'd planned.

THE LINDHOLM'S YARD was crowded with buggies when Jack returned a scant half hour later in his rental car. He'd intended to take his portable computer into one of the upstairs bedrooms, but he changed his mind when he entered the kitchen and heard the noise level inside the house. There were quilts, women and children everywhere. Rebecca was in the center of the activity, directing work on one quilt, admiring another. Ruth had baby Andy—who was awake again—in her arms and was busy showing him off to all their guests. "Did you get your business worked out?" Ruth asked.

Suddenly all eyes were upon him. Jack saw a few speculative smiles, a few more blushes, and knew from the way some of the women were trying not to giggle that they'd all been talking about him—and probably Rebecca—before he got back. "Sort of," he said, feeling ill at ease in the midst of so much female activity. "I'm going to have to write a new scene." A new love scene. "I wonder..." Jack cast Ruth a hopeful glance. He knew he would never make his deadline if he didn't have help with Andy. "If you wouldn't mind watching Andy for a few hours more..."

"It's no problem. I enjoy taking care of the little one," Ruth said.

"Well, then, I'll just find a quiet place to work," Jack said. Apparently it was not going to be anywhere inside the plain white clapboard farmhouse. Jack looked at Rebecca. "Any suggestions?"

She smiled back brightly, the look in her eyes too innocent to be believed as she suggested softly, "I suppose you could rent a room in a nearby inn."

"I'd rather stay here," he said. With you.

"Then you might try the barn."

"REBECCA IS DOING THIS to me on purpose," Jack told the cow in the stall below as he carried the laptop computer and then two thick quilts up the ladder and into the spacious loft. He descended the ladder again and headed for the express package containing his notes. "Trying to make me want to leave, or at the very least take Andy and move to a hotel where I could work in comfort, but I'm telling you it is not going to work."

The cow looked at him with big liquid-brown eyes and went on chewing her cud. "Okay," Jack said as he paused before the stall, "so maybe it's a little crazy, me working out here like this when I have a luxurious home with a fully outfitted writing studio at home, but I've always said a true writer can work anywhere. This isn't so different from working on location. I once wrote a scene in the middle of a jungle. Did I tell you that? No, guess not." And what am I doing talking to a cow anyway, he thought as he headed for the ladder once again and climbed up into the loft. He sighed as he tried to get comfortable.

"Maybe Rebecca's right. Maybe I am losing it," he said softly to himself. The only thing he knew for certain was that he wasn't leaving here until he'd made Rebecca admit her feelings for him, and for their baby, and he didn't care how long it took. So long as he accomplished his mission by the end of the week, in time to get back to his job.

Down below, the cow let out a soft moo. Ignoring his surroundings, Jack spread out one blanket, wrapped the other around his shoulders and began to type. The words came slowly at first, but soon picked up speed.

"IT'S BEEN HOURS since you took Jack his dinner," Ruth said worriedly to Rebecca as 9:00 p.m. approached. "Maybe you should go out and check on him."

"I'm sure he's fine. He's just working hard on his writing." In fact, he had been so absorbed in his work he had hardly noticed her, Rebecca fumed. He'd merely mumbled a distracted thank-you as she handed him his supper tray, and then resumed typing.

"Well, I'm going to bed," Eli said.

"I'll be up in a minute, too," Ruth said. She turned back to Rebecca. "Do you think we should take the baby up with us?" She looked at Andy, sleeping peacefully in his cradle.

Rebecca thought about taking care of the baby herself, then recalling the assumptions Jack had jumped to when she'd simply sung a lullaby to him, decided against it. "I think that would be a good idea," she said firmly. She stood and went to get her black wool cloak down from the coatrack next to the door. "In the meantime, I'll go out and check on Jack. There's really no reason for him to continue working in the barn now, when it's so quiet in here."

Ruth nodded. She and Eli ascended the stairs as Rebecca lit one of the kerosene lanterns and headed out to the barn. The cadence of the tapping computer keys continued unabated as she hung the lantern on a hook near the center support post, climbed the ladder and moved into the loft. "I would've thought you'd be finished by now," Rebecca said. "But then I had no idea you'd be building yourself an office out here."

Jack swung around to face her. He, too, had hung a lantern up on a peg so he could see. In the soft glow of the lamp, he looked a little like a pirate, his hair all tousled, an evening beard shadowing his face. Rebecca would have died before admitting it to him, but she was glad he had done more than grunt at her this time.

"Like it, hmm?" Jack asked.

She stepped inside the "room" he'd made by stacking bales of hay three high around the perimeter. The stacked hay effectively blocked any drafts and made a cozy work space.

Additional bales of hay, stacked one and two high, served as his writing chair and desk. He had covered both with a quilt, and laid another one on the loft floor. "You've been busy since I was out here at suppertime," Rebecca said.

"Yeah, well, it started getting cold when the sun went down, but I was on a roll, so I really didn't want to move. I just went with it, you know?"

Rebecca nodded. "I feel the same way when I'm blocking out a quilt," she said. "When I begin to see a new design in my head, I want to lay out all the pieces, fast, and baste them together, before I forget. If I can't do that, then I draw a sketch."

Jack grinned. "You do understand. I guess our work isn't so different after all."

Silence fell between them. Rebecca glanced at the portable printer next to the portable computer. "Is that hard to work?"

"Nope. Want me to teach you?"

Yes, Rebecca thought, but she knew it would be frowned on. Computers weren't Amish, even New Order Amish. She frowned, wondering if she would ever stop feeling caught between two worlds.

Jack continued to regard her silently as he took the red correcting pen he'd stuck behind his ear and tossed it down into the hay. "What time is it, anyway?"

"After nine. My grandparents have already gone to bed. They took Andy up with them."

"He was asleep already?"

"The quilting bee wore him out."

"I can understand that," Jack teased. "You women were a noisy bunch."

Rebecca grinned, looking at the several small stacks of paper he had lined up on his makeshift desk. "You're still not finished yet?"

"No." He frowned and stretched his long legs out in front of him. "But I am due for a break."

Rebecca felt odd standing when he was sitting. She perched on the edge of a bale in the corner and folded her hands primly in her lap. "I never imagined writing would be such hard work."

"There are days when it isn't and days when it is." Jack rubbed the tense muscles in the back of his neck. "Today is one of those days when it is."

Rebecca looked back at the pages. She couldn't help it. She wanted to read them and see what he had written. She contented herself with asking a few more questions instead. "You said you had one more scene to write?" Jack nodded. "How many pages is one scene?"

"For this particular one, about ten pages."

Rebecca blinked. "It took you that long to write only ten pages?"

"No." Jack shook his head and sighed again. "It's a love scene. I'm having trouble getting the words right. So I keep doing it over and over. When I get one I'm completely happy with, I'll send it on to Los Angeles."

"I see," Rebecca said quietly.

Jack doubted that. In fact, he was sure she had no idea how tough it had been for him, hanging out here most of the day and all of the evening, trying to keep his mind on the characters in his movie when all he could really think about was Rebecca and how much he wanted to make love to her up here, the required revisions of the pivotal love scene for the movie be damned. Worse, he was stiff and sore from the hours spent hunched over the hay in the cool barn, working under primitive conditions so he wouldn't have to leave Rebecca. So she wouldn't think he was running off and deserting her again.

"What are you thinking?" she asked quietly.

"How glad I am that you came out to interrupt me again," Jack teased. "And I'm sorry I didn't pay you any attention earlier."

Rebecca glanced at his empty dinner tray. "I see you ate your dinner anyway."

"One of my many talents, eating and typing at the same time," he said with a grin, wishing she didn't look so damn good. He got up to see if there was any more lemonade in the thermos she'd brought out. There was just enough for half a cup each. He poured his into his glass and hers in the cup that topped the thermos. Walking over to hand her the cup, he sat down next to her on the hay. With the black cloak wrapped around her shoulders, feathery wisps of blond hair escaping from beneath her kapp, her cheeks pink with embarrassment, she had never looked prettier, or more ripe for seduction.

"So..." he said as she sipped wordlessly from the cup, "what brings you out here?" It was funny, but he had never seen her look so shy, so like she wanted to simply be with him.

Rebecca swallowed. "I came to check on you before I went to bed." She stood hastily, as if just remembering she had interrupted his work. "I can see you're fine," she continued briskly, bending to put the cup aside, "so I'll be leaving."

"Wait a minute." He caught her wrist and pulled her down onto the quilt beside him, on the makeshift bench seat. "I've got a question for you—on the Amish." He wished he could take her hair down again. He loved the way it felt in his hands, silky soft, deeply waving...

She regarded him suspiciously. Beside him, he felt her thigh tense. "What kind of question?"

Jack sighed inwardly. He could tell by the look on her face that all her defenses had just snapped securely back into place. So much for wooing her, at least tonight. And since that was the case, he might as well get back to work. "Have you ever bundled with anyone? You know, carried on a courtship on opposite sides of a bed?"

Rebecca's fair brows lowered like thunderclouds over her light blue eyes. "Bundling went out of use years ago for most Amish sects."

"How come?" Jack interrupted.

Rebecca drew in a deep breath that lifted her breasts and let it out slowly. She looked past him, toward the sturdy beams overhead. "Many of the bishops felt it led to amoral behavior."

It sure did in the movie scene he was writing, Jack thought. Too bad it wouldn't here. But, as long as she was out here, he might as well make use of the chance to have someone help him visualize what he was trying to write. He drained the thermos and put it aside. Taking her hand, he guided her to her feet and led her to the center of the blanket he had laid out on the loft floor. She looked down at the quilt he had rolled up and stretched lengthwise in the center of the blanket. "Don't tell me," she drawled, "this is your bundling place."

He grinned back at her, feeling ridiculously happy despite the poor work conditions and the pressure of having to write such a pivotal scene under incredible time pressure. "You catch on quick. Anyway, since I'm having such a hard time trying to envision this bundling scene I was hoping you'd help me out."

"Help you out how?" Rebecca ground out.

"All you have to do is pretend to bundle with me for a little while, up here in the loft," Jack explained. The moment the words were out, he knew his motives were less than pure. From a technical standpoint, he really didn't need to see Rebecca stretched out beside him on the quilt to be able to write the scene. But he did need another kiss. Or maybe two or three...

"You know, Jack, I thought you were crazy before but now I'm sure of it," Rebecca said. "You have taken leave of your senses." She started to step past him.

Again, he caught her wrist and tugged her close. "Afraid bundling with me would lead to amoral behavior?" he teased softly, taunting her with his gaze.

As he had expected she would, the challenge in his voice got to her. "Don't flatter yourself, Jack," she said stiffly. "I was a fool once. I do not intend to be one again."

He studied her flushed cheeks. He wasn't sure whether this was the time to get her to admit her feelings for him or not. He did know they were running out of time. And they had damn few chances to be alone. This opportunity had been handed to him as if it were a gift; he'd be foolish not to use it. Particularly when it might lead to her accepting the inevitability of their love. Or admitting to him the truth about their Andy.

"Then prove you're immune to me," he taunted softly, keeping his eyes on hers, "and bundle with me for a little while."

She sucked in a quick angry breath. "This is ridiculous."

Jack just shrugged. The gauntlet had already been thrown down, it was up to her to pick it up. She didn't disappoint him. "Fine. We'll bundle," she said tightly. She stepped to one side of the quilt he had spread out over the loft floor, and reclined next to the rolled-up quilt in the middle, her body as stiff and straight as a stick. "This is my side." Rebecca pointed to the right. "That's yours."

Jack wasted no time taking his place on the other side of the "bundling bed" in the loft. Hands folded behind his neck, he lay back on his side, a grin on his face. "So," Jack said, wondering what the hell people did talk about in those days, "how did the quilting bee go?"

"We finished five more quilts. They'll each bring about two hundred dollars at market—"

"Is that all?" he interrupted, rolling onto his side. He propped his elbow up and rested his head on his hand. "They'd bring at least three hundred and fifty, maybe more, in Los Angeles."

"Yes," Rebecca corrected him with exaggerated patience, "but I don't live in Los Angeles."

"Well, there you're in luck, Rebecca, because I do."

"It's not going to work, Jack," Rebecca huffed as she hastened to sit up. Her expression was tense and accusing as she twisted around to face him. "You're not going to trick me into going out there with you."

"Hey." Irritated to be falsely accused, Jack caught her and rolled so she was beneath him. "I am not trying to trick you into doing anything," he said, bracing his arms on either side of her and staring down into her face.

"Aren't you?"

"No," he said quietly, threading his hands through her hair, pushing her kapp back, off her head. Needing to see her hair down, just for a little while, he began undoing the braid. "I'm not. I would never hurt you. Don't you know that?" he asked softly, combing his fingers through the silky white blond strands.

Rebecca's lower lip trembled. "Oh, Jack." Tears of regret and longing filled her eyes. "I wish things were different. I wish things could work for us, but they can't," she said in a choked voice as she struggled to get up once again.

He pushed her back. They'd come this far. She wasn't backing off now. Not if he had anything to say about it. "You haven't given us a chance to work things out," he said firmly, "but it's high time you did."

In a flash, she knew what he intended. And he knew what she intended. Before she could so much as try to scramble away from him again, he had both her wrists in his hands, and had pinned them above her head. Her breath caught in her chest. Her heart raced. Lower still, there was a mounting tension deep inside her. "Jack, don't—" She struggled against him, to no avail.

"Don't what?" he asked as his lips touched her cheeks, her brow, her eyes. He had never known he was capable of such tenderness. But around Rebecca, around Andy, all he felt was the incredible overwhelming desire to love.

Rebecca drew in a tremulous breath. "Don't... do... this."

"Don't do what?" Jack asked as he felt her body soften in surrender against the length of his. He kissed her eyelids shut, then worked his way down her cheek to her lips. His mouth hovered above hers as her eyelids fluttered open once again. "Don't kiss you?" His lips touched hers lightly, rubbed across them sensually, then withdrew. His smile widened rapaciously. "Or don't French-kiss you?"

"Jack—"

He cut off her gasp with a deep, sensual kiss. Electricity leapt and sizzled between them. "Tell me you don't want me," Jack challenged as the aching in his groin intensified and he kissed his way down her throat, to the collar of her dress. "Tell me you want me to leave this farm right now, leave and never come back, and I will." Ready to make good on his promise, he let go of her wrists. Bracing his weight on the forearms he'd planted on either side of her, he looked down into her face.

"Or, tell me you want me, that you've always wanted me, and we'll figure out a way to be together from now on." He paused, silently willing her to do the right thing for them both. "It's your choice, Rebecca. You decide."

Her eyes held his. Now was the moment of truth, Rebecca thought. And as she looked into his dark blue eyes, she knew she couldn't evade him any longer. "I should tell you to go," she said as her heart took up a slow, deliberate rhythm in her chest. She touched a hand to his thick chestnut hair. "But I can't." A familiar bittersweet longing filled her soul. "Not until I kiss you one last time." It might not be much, she thought miserably, but it was all she was going to have in the lonely days to come. The moment she had seen Jack get that express package she had known that he would be leaving her. It was just a matter of time now.

Jack's eyes darkened, as if he knew all she felt, and more, felt the impending loss, too. "Then one more kiss is what you've got," he said softly, lowering his mouth to hers.

The cautious part of her meant to hold him at bay, keep him from deepening the kiss unnecessarily, or going any farther than that, but the moment his lips touched hers again all was lost. All Rebecca could think about, all she could feel, all she could want, was the wonder of his mouth, and the incredibly sensual, incredibly giving way it felt, moving over her lips. She had never felt so much a woman, as she did at that moment, never wanted so much to be one with a man, and that made it all the harder to draw away.

Disappointment coiled sharply inside Jack as Rebecca slipped from beneath him. Tensing with an immediate, galvanizing sense of loss, he reached out and curled a hand around her waist. "Don't go, Rebecca," he said softly, feeling both surprised and annoyed by the raw need he heard in his own low voice. He'd thought he'd stopped being vulnerable the day he'd been old enough to realize that his own father had walked out on him and his mother without so much as a second thought. But here he was, again sounding like a needy kid. "Please."

Rebecca struggled into her cloak. She looked very close to tears herself. "I have to. My grandparents might wake. And if they do, they'll wonder what's been keeping me."

Jack sighed. Things weren't exactly simple now, but they could be, he thought, if only he and Rebecca had the courage to be completely honest with her grandparents. "Then let's tell them," he said.

Chapter Ten

"Are you crazy?" Rebecca asked, her voice rising emotionally in the silence of the loft. Down below, a sleepy cow mooed in irritation.

Rolling his eyes at the interruption, Jack continued to regard Rebecca seriously. "Ruth and Eli should know we care about each other."

Rebecca gave him a searing look. "We don't, not in the way you seem to be implying," she corrected as she smoothed the rumpled layers of plain cotton chemise, blue dress and black apron. Love was something that came after years of knowing someone, after you'd seen them at their best and their worst and still cared deeply what happened to them. She and Jack hadn't even known each other a week, all told.

"No?" Jack countered, just as acerbically. "Then what do you call what's been going on here?"

She should have known he would ask that! Rebecca glanced around for her cloak, wondering where she had left it. "Infatuation!"

Jack shook his head. He watched her snatch up her cloak, then caught her hand as she tried to pass him.

"We feel a lot more than a simple infatuation for each other, Rebecca," he corrected sternly, swinging her back around in front of him as if she were a partner in a barn dance.

Rebecca tipped up her chin belligerently as her knees collided with the muscular solidness of his. "No, we don't, Jack. You're just too much of a romantic to admit it at the moment." He quirked a brow at her; she quirked hers back, even more haughtily, then withdrew her hand from his and stepped back. "I am sure you'll come to grips with the reality of the situation in due time. Maybe as soon as you leave Pennsylvania." Jack gave her another quelling look that flamed her temper even more. Unable to help herself, Rebecca added caustically, "At least until another unclaimed child of yours appears on Alec Roman's doorstep."

Jack moved to the left, blocking her exit from the makeshift office. "That was uncalled for, Rebecca."

"Hey." She tapped an index finger against her breastbone, then pointed it back at him in an accusing manner. "I'm not the one sowing my seed all over this country."

Jack's mouth tightened in a grim warning that would have made a less spirited woman back off, but not Rebecca. "That was also uncalled for," he said, closing the distance between them swiftly.

Before she could do much more than mutter a protest, he took her into his arms again and held her close. Warmth flowed through her, followed swiftly by desire. Her blood quickened at every pulse point. It would be so easy to let herself be seduced into making love with him again, Rebecca thought. Too easy.

Sighing wearily, she lifted her chin to his. Light blue eyes met dark blue. "Let me ask you a question, Jack," she said, prefacing it with silent reassurances that she was adult enough to handle the answer. "Are you going back to Los Angeles?"

Jack's eyes darkened to a midnight-blue and he frowned, his reluctance to talk about that underscored only by his reluctance to let her go. "I'm going to have to, in a few days," he said, making no effort to spare her from harsh reality. "But you could come with me and Andy," he continued swiftly. "You could visit—"

Visit. Her heart sinking, Rebecca twisted out of his arms. "Maybe if you lived in the next county, Jack," she said in weary resignation, trying her hardest to be adult about all this. "But you live all the way across the country."

Jack watched her distance herself from him even more. He followed her over to the quilt where her kapp had fallen, watched as she took a seat on the bundle of hay and began to smooth her hair with her fingers. Jack removed the comb he habitually carried in his back pocket and flipped it onto her lap. "Well, we all don't drive buggies, you know," he reminded her in a deadpan voice. "You could hop a train or a bus. Hell, you could even live dangerously and hop a plane."

"And pay for it with what? My family is barely getting by as it is. They're going to need every cent I can bring in from the sale of my quilts just to buy the spring seed.''

Jack paused. ''I had no idea . . .'' he said in a low, worried tone.

Rebecca put both hands out in front of her to ward off any further sympathy or comment. ''I shouldn't have said anything. I'm just frustrated because it's getting increasingly hard to make a living off the land. Our taxes go up every year. Some years it's all we can do to pay them.''

''Then why do you stay?''

Rebecca ran the comb through her hair, then began to pleat it into a single braid at the back of her head. ''Because it's my home.''

Again, Jack shook his head. His jaw hardened pugnaciously. ''Home is where the heart is, Rebecca.''

''Meaning what?'' Rebecca secured her braid to the back of her head with a pin, then put her kapp back on. ''I'm supposed to move to L.A. with you until you tire of me?''

''I will never tire of you,'' he stated. ''But that's the gist of my proposal, yeah.''

Rebecca couldn't believe he thought she had so little going in her life that she would just drop everything to be with him until he tired of her. This wasn't a movie he was scripting. ''Well, forget it!'' she stormed back.

''Why?'' he asked again in a low mesmerizing tone, laced with quiet reason.

"Because it's not going to happen, Jack." She could not remember ever feeling quite so melancholy. "I desire you." Her lower lip trembled. "I admit it. But I'm not going to let you romanticize this," she said, her low voice gathering strength as all her self-protective forces moved firmly into place. "I'm not going to let you romanticize us, Jack."

He was silent, studying her thoughtfully. "The way your ex-husband did?" he asked gently.

Rebecca slipped her cloak on with stiff, jerky movements. "His intentions were honorable in the beginning, too."

The aggravation she'd seen on his face earlier was back. "Don't assume Wesley Adair and I are the same just because we're both English," he said.

He was acting as if her view of the situation was the only problem they had to surmount. "Then you stop romanticizing me and see me as who I really am."

"And who are you, Rebecca?" Jack demanded without quarter, his expression pensive. "Are you Amish or English or half of both? Admit it, Rebecca, you're not just confused about us, you're confused about you."

His words hit home. She sensed admitting the truth in them, however, would leave her at a distinct disadvantage. "Why would I be confused about myself?" she asked coolly. She sat perched on the edge of the bale of hay. She had been away from the house too long, but this was a conversation better held here, and she could tell from the look on his face, Jack wasn't about to let it go.

He sat beside her on the bale of hay. He lifted her hand and put it on his thigh, his warm strong fingers covering her cold limp ones. "Because you've always straddled two worlds, really belonging in neither place," he said softly, his dark blue eyes as persuasive as they were probing. "Part of you must rail at some of the hardships of Amish life."

Rebecca's hand tensed in his. She swallowed around the knot of growing emotion in her throat. As always, Jack was seeing far more about her than she was comfortable with. "So what?" she retorted quietly, her low voice echoing in the stillness of the barn. Shadows from the kerosene lantern hanging on the hook danced on the sturdy walls and rafters. "Everyone has frustrations."

Jack gently touched the back of his hand to her cheek. "But not every Amish woman makes reckless love with me." The silence strung out between them. His voice lowered a seductive notch. They looked at each other, each struggling to understand the other's feelings and needs. "I'm not asking you to give up all that much," he said finally.

Wasn't he? Following him to Los Angeles would mean giving up her entire life here, and that was a risk she just couldn't take. The people in the community had forgiven her for making a fool of herself over an Englishman once. If she did it a second time, to the same result, she'd be considered a woman of loose morals. And though she might not care so very much what other people thought about her, she knew her grandparents did, and she couldn't bear to see them hurt like that.

Rebecca stood and restlessly moved away. The loft felt cold and damp. As lonely and desolate as her heart. She stared at the shadow of herself on the wall, and the outline her cloak made. When she had regained her composure, she turned back to face him. "This isn't a movie, Jack. It's real life, with real people, all of whom stand to be very hurt if this thing blows up in our faces."

"How do you know?" He got to his feet in one slow, smooth movement that in no way undermined the intensity of his gaze. "I think your grandparents would understand why the three of us need to be together now if we just leveled with Ruth and Eli and told them the truth. In fact, I think under the circumstances they'd want us to be together."

"You're wrong, Jack. My grandparents would think I was a fool if I ran off with you. And they'd be right," she said, moving closer as she pleaded her case. "Things don't work out neatly just because the writer in you thinks they should."

"Oh, I don't know about that," he quipped lightly. "I think I scripted this last scene up here pretty well."

Rebecca's face burned as the sensual memories returned. She refused to let him get her off the subject at hand. "You have to face it, Jack," she continued. Melancholy flooded her once again. "As much as we desire each other, a love affair between us would never work long-term because of the differences in our lifestyles and our backgrounds."

His brows rose in the equivalent of a shrug. "Says you," he disagreed.

"I am not going to have another failed marriage," she said flatly, her temper flaring as her attempts to reason with him failed.

Jack folded his arms in front of him. He waggled his eyebrows at her and grinned as if he'd just won a major battle. "So you're thinking marriage, huh, Rebecca?" he teased. "I take that as a very good sign."

Rebecca stormed past him and gathered up the dinner tray. "This is all a game to you," she said bad temperedly, annoyed he had gotten her to reveal so much more about her feelings for him than she had ever intended. Annoyed he had made her hope they might have a future together one day after all.

He stepped aside to let her pass. His eyes gleamed in the shadows of the barn. "It's not a game, Rebecca. It's real life, just like Andy is a real baby, not a figment of my imagination."

Her back stiff, Rebecca halted in her tracks.

"I'm not giving up on you," he said as she turned around slowly to face him. He gave her a steely look. "Nor on us. Not now and not ever. And the sooner you accept that the happier you'll be."

"SO, YOU SENT YOUR WORK back to Los Angeles?" Ruth said the next morning when Jack walked inside.

Jack shrugged out of his leather jacket and took a seat next to the quilt the women had spread out on the floor. Andy was lying on his back, his head turned to the Amish rag doll Rebecca had made for him. Only it wasn't the same doll he had seen the other night. Rebecca had embroidered two blue eyes, a turned-up nose, pink circle cheeks, a smattering of freckles and a big smile on the doll. She'd also used yellow yarn for hair, and made a black felt Amish hat to go with the blue shirt and black overalls on the boy doll. It was an Amish version of Raggedy Andy. And Andy seemed as taken by the love she'd put into it as he was. "Yes," Jack answered Ruth in a distracted tone. He paused to smile at Rebecca's grandmother over his shoulder. "I just faxed it."

"Your employers were happy with your work?" Ruth asked.

"I hope so," Jack said. The pages were among the best he'd ever written. After Rebecca had left him alone last night, it had only taken him another hour to polish the dialogue he'd already had and add the finishing touches such as scene direction. He'd wanted to be available to Rebecca today and spend time with her again. Unfortunately she wasn't sparing him any attention.

Instead she was busy blocking out yet another quilt at the kitchen table. This one was a series of triple chains and random stars and octagons. She'd used every color of the rainbow in the design. Ruth kept glancing at Rebecca's work, intrigued, and Jack knew exactly how she felt. He couldn't seem to stop looking at the quilt Rebecca was designing, either. It was almost too pretty, too unique to be used as a comforter on a bed. He felt it should be hanging in an art gallery somewhere.

Rebecca met his gaze equably. "I imagine you're about ready to go back to Los Angeles then."

"On the contrary," Jack said, mocking her almost too pleasant tone, and saw the change in her eyes. "In fact, I'm thinking of staying a few more days. That is, if it's all right with Ruth and Eli."

Ruth smiled back at him as she finished filling a wicker basket with jars of home-canned peaches. "Of course it's all right, Jack." She shut the lid on the picnic hamper and reached for her black cloak and matching bonnet. As she tied her bonnet under her chin, she said, "We've enjoyed having you here. Now if the two of you will excuse me," she said, noting that Eli had parked the horse and buggy just outside the back door, "I've got to take these peaches and the strudel Rebecca just baked to Mrs. Good."

Rebecca continued arranging quilting squares long after her grandparents had left. Jack let her revel in the silence for several minutes as he played with the son he'd spent precious little time with the past twenty-four hours. Finally he decided it was time they cleared the air. "Still mad at me, aren't you?" he said.

Rebecca threaded a needle and then began the process of basting the squares together with long smooth stitches. "Anger is a waste of both time and energy, Jack."

Jack stood and sauntered over to the table. "So you're happy with me then?" he teased.

She gave him a droll look he found greatly encouraging.

"Come see our son," he said. Taking her by the hand, he tugged her to the edge of the blanket where Andy was still playing contentedly. After a moment's hesitation, she dropped her eyes from his and glanced at Andy. He was curling his tiny fingers toward the doll she had made for him. He batted it frantically, finally curling his fingers around the doll's hand. "See how much he likes the doll you made for him?" Jack asked softly, tightening his own grip on Rebecca's hand, noting that she hadn't moved to extricate herself from his hold—yet.

Rebecca sighed. The sound was wistful in the quiet of the room. "He likes the face I sewed on it," she said in a clipped tone of voice.

Jack tugged her down so that they were both sitting picnic style on the edge of Andy's quilt.

"I wish someone had sewed me a doll like this when I was a kid."

Rebecca's light blue eyes widened curiously. "What kind of toys did you have?" she asked.

Jack shrugged. Maybe he shouldn't have started this conversation. "Just things you could buy in a store. Bats and balls, stuff like that."

Rebecca's teeth scraped the softness of her lower lip. "That's the first time I've ever heard you say anything about your childhood."

Now Jack knew he shouldn't have started this. "Not much to tell."

Rebecca's glance held with mesmerizing intensity. "Not much to tell or not much you want to tell?" she asked.

Touché, Jack thought. "What do you want to know?" he asked gruffly, wishing this weren't so hard for him.

Rebecca's blue eyes narrowed speculatively. "Did you have a happy childhood?"

Jack held himself very still, wondering if he should give her the cheerful version he had cleaned up for strangers or the ugly, unvarnished truth. He looked into her eyes and decided on a point in between. "What I remember most about the early years is being very lonely. I think that's why I became a writer. I didn't have a lot to occupy myself, so I had to use my vivid imagination to keep myself entertained."

"No brothers or sisters?"

"No," Jack said, aware the two of them had that in common, being only children. "Though I've got a couple of friends—Alec Roman and Grady Noland, who feel like brothers."

"What was it like for you, growing up?"

"Finances were really tight. My mother had to work two jobs just to support us, which in turn meant I rarely saw her. If it hadn't been for the scholarship to prep school, and the one to Penn after that, who knows where I would've ended up?" Jack looked at Andy, who was still gazing contentedly at his Amish doll, and promised his son would have a better life than he'd had.

Rebecca studied Jack with compassion and understanding. "But you're happy writing, aren't you?"

"Very."

Her expression turned troubled. "What's it like to live in California? Los Angeles is very trendy, isn't it?" Jack nodded, not sure where this was going. He was sure he didn't like it. "Fashions change constantly, don't they?"

Jack shrugged. "I guess. I always dress pretty much the same. Jeans, shirts, leather jacket. Sometimes I add a bill cap or vary the shoes, but—" he held his arms akimbo "—what you see now is pretty much what you get, at least as far as my wardrobe is concerned."

She flushed and looked irritated again. "You know what I mean."

Jack touched his son lightly on the cheek and watched him smile, then drew a deep breath. "I think I know what you're getting at. I think you're trying to convince me you wouldn't fit in there. You're wasting your time, Rebecca. Because I think you would." Still sitting on the edge of the quilt, he lowered his mouth and kissed her sweetly. She was trembling when they drew apart and Jack knew exactly how she felt. He wanted nothing more than to say to hell with everything and everyone and make love to her then and there. Only Andy's playful gurgling reminded him they couldn't.

He released her slowly and turned his attention back to his son. The son Rebecca still wouldn't claim.

She was already getting to her feet. Her steps brisk and purposeful, she moved across the kitchen to get her cloak. He watched her take the car keys off the hook next to the back door. "Please keep an eye on the stew," she said.

Jack tensed as beside him Andy kicked and flailed, trying to get the doll to do the same. "Where are you going?"

Rebecca turned to face him, her expression brisk and purposeful. "It's my day to pick up quilts. I'll be taking the car."

Jack picked up Andy and the doll and held both cradled in his arms. "I could drive you," he offered. Andy would probably enjoy riding in a car again.

Rebecca looked at him. "No, Jack," she said softly but firmly, "you can't drive me. There's too much talk about us already."

"SHE SHOULD HAVE BEEN back by now, shouldn't she?" Jack asked as seven o'clock came and went.

Eli and Ruth looked as disturbed as he felt. "It isn't like Rebecca to miss supper with the family," Eli agreed.

Ruth paced to the window. A light snow had begun to fall. "Perhaps the bad weather is slowing her down," she said.

"Or perhaps she is having trouble with her car again," Eli said with a frown.

"Why?" Jack asked, the anxiety of not knowing what had happened to Rebecca almost more than he could bear. "What's wrong with her car? She's got snow chains on it, doesn't she?"

"Of course she has snow chains, as well as snow tires." Eli frowned. "But the radiator has a leak in it.

We patched it last month, but…it is possible the cold weather has ruined the patch."

Might have ruined the patch? It was all Jack could do not to swear as he imagined the many calamities that might have befallen Rebecca. His heart racing, he handed Andy over to Ruth. "I'm going to go out and look for her," he announced, already reaching for his leather jacket. He shrugged it on then searched his pockets for his keys. "Do you have any idea which roads she might have taken?"

Eli nodded. He seemed glad Jack was taking action. "I'll write you a list," he said.

Minutes later, Jack set out in his rental car, the map in his hand. The snow made it almost impossible to see more than a few feet in front of him. Worse, because of the weather, few cars were on the road. What if he couldn't find her? What if her car had broken down somewhere and she had been mugged trying to fix it? What if she had been in an accident? He had to stop this, he schooled himself firmly.

Finally he saw her old station wagon. It was pulled over to the side of the road. The emergency flashers were on but it was apparently otherwise intact, he noted with relief. Eli had probably been right. It probably was the radiator.

He parked behind her, turned on his emergency flashers and got out. He strode to the car window, the snow pelting his face. Before he got to her side, Rebecca had opened her car door and stepped out. "Jack!" She looked happy but not particularly surprised to see him. It irritated him to see that she was as calm as her grandparents had been. They were all acting as if this kind of calamity happened every day. Then again, considering the antiquated condition of the car she drove, it probably did.

"What happened?" he asked, not sure whether he wanted to shake her or kiss her. Only that he was very glad to see her all in one piece.

"What do you think?" She scowled at him in obvious irritation as tiny snowflakes pelted her fair cheeks. "My car quit on me."

Jack's frown deepened at her flip tone. It irked him no end that Rebecca never seemed to sense when she was in danger. For a woman her age, she had a serious lack of street sense. Whereas he, having grown up in a very bad part of Philadelphia, had an overabundance of it. "Why didn't you tell me the radiator on it was bad when you left this afternoon?" he demanded irascibly.

She sighed, exasperated, and planted her hands on her hips. "Because it was working then."

"But not now."

She shot him a deadpan look. "Obviously not or I wouldn't be sitting here on the side of the road not moving now, would I, oh handsome rescuer?"

Jack couldn't help but grin at her teasing description of him. He rubbed a hand through his hair. "I see that tart tongue of yours is still in working order," he said finally.

"Yep."

He glanced at the back of the station wagon. As before when he had rescued her, the car was piled high with hand-sewn quilts. "I suppose you want to move the quilts from your car to mine?" he said.

"We're leaving my car here?" she asked in surprise.

"I'm no miracle worker with cars and I can't tow it with this rental car. So yeah, we'll have to."

Rebecca frowned, but made no further complaint. They worked in silence, rushing back and forth. Finally they finished and she got in the passenger side. He slid in beside her, behind the wheel. His heater was going full blast. It was warm and cozy inside. "You're lucky I came along," he said as he jerked off his gloves and tossed them onto the dash.

Rebecca took off her black wool bonnet and dusted the snow from the brim. "It seems to me I've heard this speech before, Jack Rourke. Someone would've come along eventually."

"A nice Amish family?"

"Of course."

"And if they hadn't?"

She shrugged. "I would have either bundled up in the quilts and waited until morning, or bundled up in the quilts and walked to the next farmhouse, depending on the weather. But first, I simply waited to be rescued."

Her logic was plain and simple. Unfortunately they lived in a complicated, often messy and dangerous world. "Dammit, Rebecca, you need to have a more reliable car if you're going to be driving around alone like this," he said, in no hurry to get back to the Lindholm farm now that he'd found her.

Incensed, she shifted to face him. "You have no right to lecture me this way."

Jack ignored the light layer of snow dusting the windshield. "I have every right."

"Because you've appointed yourself my temporary knight in shining armor?" she retorted through tightly gritted teeth.

"Because I care about you," he corrected roughly.

"That doesn't matter." She reached for the door handle and started to push from the car.

"The hell it doesn't," Jack said. He pulled her back in his arms and reached past her to shut her door all the way again. "I want you safe." Without warning, he was suddenly fed up with the tension, the waiting, the pretending they didn't want and need each other desperately. "Don't you understand, Rebecca?" he asked hoarsely. "I can't go on like this—worrying about you, how you feel. You're my world, Rebecca," he whispered, his voice catching just a little, before he clamped down hard and got control of it once again. "My whole world."

He lowered his mouth to hers and delivered a searing kiss, putting all that he felt for her, all that he had been searching for, in that one caress. He expected her to fight; she surrendered. He expected her to protest; she brought him closer and whispered his name. He shifted her onto his lap, thinking they could handle a few more kisses. But nothing in his ever-present and all too vivid imagination had ever prepared him for the touch and feel and taste of her, the sunny springlike scent of her. Nothing had ever prepared him for the highly romantic, supercharged experience of kissing Rebecca while the snow fell all around them. Their mouths blended in desperation, in joy, in longing.

Finally Rebecca broke off the kiss. "We can't go on this way, Jack," she said in a voice that trembled. "I'm not cut out for sneaking around. If someone were to drive by and see us and word of this got back to my grandparents—" She compressed her lips together. Heat flooded her face as she shook her head in wordless displeasure. "It would be just too humiliating, not just for me, but for my whole family."

Jack was silent, unable to argue with her about that. It had been years since he'd been reduced to sneaking around and stealing kisses like a love-struck teenager. "I admit I'm not comfortable with the situation, either," he said gruffly. "But there is a solution, Rebecca."

"What?" Rebecca asked, flushing as his gaze fastened on the throbbing pulse in her throat.

Jack gently tucked a hand beneath her chin, lifted her face up to his and looked deep into her eyes. "We could get married."

Chapter Eleven

"Now I know you're crazy!" Rebecca said, moving all the way over to her side of the car.

Jack turned on his headlights, switched off the emergency blinkers and backed up slightly. "Because I want us to be together?" he asked as he eased the rental car back onto the road.

"Because Andy is not my baby," Rebecca said, clamping her arms around her waist. She stared straight ahead. He sighed and braked as they approached a four-way stop.

"I told you before, Rebecca. Sending me on a wild moose chase is not going to work."

"I am not trying to get rid of you."

"Aren't you?" Jack asked as snow continued to pelt their windshield. Rebecca fell silent. "I'm sure Andy is my son, Rebecca, and no amount of clever tricks or skillful dissuasion on your part is going to convince me otherwise."

Jack checked to make sure the intersection was clear, then continued on, driving slowly and carefully as the weather warranted.

Rebecca looked out the window at the blur of white landscape passing by. Her feelings were in turmoil. She couldn't understand why Jack would not let go of this theory, that Andy was his child. Unless . . .

Jack had accused her of fibbing about Andy's parentage. For the first time, Rebecca began to wonder if maybe the reason Jack was so certain that Andy was his, was that Jack was the one who was fibbing here, and had been all along.

Was it possible he'd been with another woman shortly before or after he'd made love to her? Rebecca wondered. Some woman not so suited to motherhood? Some woman capable of leaving a baby on the doorstep for Jack? Was it possible, she thought, beginning to feel a little ill, that Jack had made love to another woman during the weeks he'd been staying at Alec Roman's Philadelphia mansion last spring?

"Let me ask you something, Jack." Rebecca swiveled toward him as Jack continued to drive slowly and carefully in the direction of the Lindholm farm. "If Andy weren't your child, and you realized that, even belatedly, would you get help from the authorities and try to discover who Andy's real parents were?"

"Of course I would," Jack said, sounding a little aggrieved that she even had to ask!

"Even though you've obviously fallen in love with him and would like nothing better than to raise him as your own," Rebecca continued bluntly.

Jack frowned and upped the windshield wipers' speed another notch. "I have no interest in stealing someone else's child from them," Jack said in an annoyed voice. He braked as they reached another four-way stop, then paused to regard her impatiently. "What's this all about? Why the questions?"

Rebecca hugged her waist. "I just needed to know, for my own peace of mind." And now she did. Jack had latched onto Andy because Andy really was his child. And since Andy wasn't her child, then Andy had to be the result of another fling, with another woman.

Had Jack come to Rebecca because he believed she was the mother? Perhaps he didn't want to own up to the fact that he had sired a child with a woman who wasn't loving and nurturing, and had come to Rebecca just because he needed a mother for Andy and figured that she fit the bill. Maybe he had been so desperate to find a mother for his son, so that Andy would not grow up with only one parent the way Jack himself had, that he was willing to do anything to convince Rebecca to step in and fill the shoes of the woman who had abandoned Andy on Alec's doorstep.

Rebecca wasn't about to be used by Jack, any more than she would marry him just so she could mother his son and have her own child to love at long last. Furthermore, Jack hadn't said anything about actually loving her, Rebecca thought. Just that he cared about her and desired her and enjoyed being with her. He had probably thrown in the idea of marriage tonight only as a last resort.

Jack braked again as they approached the next intersection. When the car came to a complete stop, he rested an arm on the steering wheel and turned toward her. "Look, Rebecca, I know having to hide the way we feel about each other is upsetting to you," he said softly, thinking erroneously that this was the reason she was so disturbed. "It's upsetting to me, too. That's why I suggested we tell your grandparents about us the other night. They already love Andy. They like me. If they knew you and I had a romantic past, too, that we wanted to make a home for Andy—"

"Hold it right there, Jack! There is no way I am publicly claiming Andy as my child," Rebecca said. "Not if that means ruining *my* reputation and the reputation of *my family* in the process!"

Again, Jack glared at her in silent frustration. "Not even if it means saving Andy from the stigma of having to grow up as an abandoned kid?" Jack asked hoarsely. He shook his head, his own painful memories surfacing once again. "I know what that's like, Rebecca. I grew up that way, too, without a father. It was hell, having to tell every single teacher I ever had that I had no idea where my father was, or if he was dead or alive, working or not. The teachers pitied me, the kids taunted me mercilessly. Is that what you want for Andy?"

"No," Rebecca said, empathetic tears spilling from her eyes. "Of course that's not what I want for Andy! No baby deserves that!"

"Then help me out here," Jack pleaded emotionally, gripping her hands with both of his. "Go to Eli and Ruth, tell them we made love last spring, that that was why you were so upset last summer and had to go away and then claim Andy as your son. Let them say they're his step-grandparents. They don't have to tell anyone in Blair County what's really going on. Just claim Andy as your own legally, so he'll have the mother that he deserves, publicly, in Los Angeles."

Rebecca moaned softly. "I can't lie about something like this, Jack."

"I'm not asking you to lie, just not tell the whole truth," Jack retorted soothingly. "We could make this work," he said softly, "if you'd give us half a chance."

Rebecca stared at Jack, unable to believe he was so naive to think they could get away with such a convoluted plan, never mind try to explain to her grandparents what had happened between Jack and her on that dark, stormy night last spring. Particularly when they didn't even really understand how it was they had fallen into bed so quickly themselves!

Jack let go of her hands abruptly and rested his arm along the back of the seat. "Look, Rebecca," he said with growing frustration, "I admit our situation has been a little mixed-up from the get-go."

"That's putting it mildly. I still can't believe I...we..." She flushed, unable to go on.

"Made love that night last spring?" he supplied softly.

"Yes!" Rebecca lowered her gaze from his.

He lifted his hand to the side of her face and gently caressed her cheek with the backs of his fingers. "Don't you see?" he asked softly in a low husky voice that sent shivers of excitement down her spine. "The speed with which we got together is proof of the fact we were meant to be together, Rebecca. And the way you feel about Andy...the way he openly responds to you and adores not just you but your entire family...is even more proof that we should be a family."

Jack made a persuasive argument. Rebecca remained on her side of the car, for a moment simply savoring the sight of him and the wonder of being alone with him in the softly falling snow. But her feelings of desire and love for him were tempered with the cold practicality in her heart, and the fear that he was using her.

She sighed as her inner anxieties obliterated the last residual feelings of pleasure she felt just being with Jack. "I confused the excitement of romance for love once Jack, and the heartbreak was almost more than I could bear. I married without a foundation of true love once. I'll never ever do it again."

"What about Andy?" Jack asked in a strangled tone. He looked even more distressed.

Rebecca steeled her heart against his emotional pleas. "I won't ruin my own family's reputation," she warned.

He touched her hair, stroked it gently. "Just think about accepting the responsibility for Andy and raising him as your own for a few more days before you give me an answer, Rebecca," he said softly. "That's all I ask."

"WHAT DID ABRAHAM SAY?" Eli asked when Rebecca and Jack returned to the farm late the next morning. They'd spent the morning having her car towed to an Amish neighbor's barn while Ruth and Eli stayed home, saw to the chores and took care of Andy.

Rebecca slipped off her cloak and hung it on the hook next to the door. She met her grandfather's eyes, hating to be the one who always had to deliver the bad news. "He said that I am going to have to buy a new radiator if I want to fix my car," she said quietly. Beside her, Jack shrugged out of his coat, too. He walked over to check on his son, who was cozily ensconced in Ruth's arms, drawing on a bottle of formula.

Ruth looked up from the baby in her arms and sent Rebecca a worried glance. "How much will that cost?"

Rebecca bit her lip. "Five hundred dollars." As her grandparents' faces grew ashen, she hastened to add, "He'll do the labor for free."

"Unfortunately," Eli said with another frown, "we don't have five hundred extra dollars to spend on the car."

Nor a way to get her quilts to market, Rebecca thought, and without the money the sale of the quilts would bring, there would be no way to buy the spring seed.

"I know a way you could get it," Jack suggested.

Everyone turned to look at him. "I've got a friend in California, Russ Saunders, who owns an art gallery that specializes in regional folk art. He's got a group of women in Appalachia who supply him with quilts on a regular basis."

"I don't see what that has to do with us," Rebecca interrupted.

"You could sell your quilts there for twice the money you'd get in Philadelphia," Jack continued. "You'd probably have enough to buy the spring seed and fix your car."

"But how would I get them there?" Rebecca asked. Shipping things was expensive. And risky. Packages on trucks had been known to get damaged. For some of the women in her quilting circle, one quilt, and the profits from it, was all they had. Others, like Rebecca, had three to five handmade quilts each to sell.

Jack appeared thoughtful as he stared down at his son, who seemed to be getting sleepier by the minute. "I have to go back to Los Angeles anyway." He paused and looked up at Rebecca. The gentle protectiveness in his eyes stirred her more than she wanted to admit.

"I could accompany you, see you got there safely and put you on a plane back home. I know," Jack hastened to add, as he turned to Eli and Ruth, seeking permission. "Normally flying isn't encouraged among the Amish, but it is permitted under special circumstances."

Ruth looked at Eli.

"Surely this qualifies," Jack continued persuasively. And just that quickly, it seemed, it was all arranged.

"YOU CHANGED CLOTHES," Jack said with a frown when Rebecca emerged from the ladies' room in the Philadelphia airport the next morning.

Rebecca grinned back at him smugly. She was wearing faded straight-leg jeans, a plain navy blue turtleneck and a bone-colored stadium jacket. She'd taken off her kapp and brushed her hair down. She wore Keds and plain white socks on her feet.

This was more of a test than he knew. "Feeling your fantasies fade, Jack?" she taunted as she switched her old-fashioned valise to her other hand.

Jack put a hand to the small of her back and guided her toward the gate. "I didn't know you had clothes like this."

Rebecca slanted a glance at Andy, who was securely strapped into a sling-style baby carrier that Jack wore like a backpack in front of him. He was wide-awake, and curiously looking around at the activity in the airport. Catching Rebecca's glance, Andy beamed her a toothless smile. Like his father, she thought on a wistful sigh, baby Andy was all charm.

Aware Jack was still waiting for an answer about where she'd gotten the clothes, Rebecca glanced up at him. "I told you I lived English the entire year I was married."

"You kept the clothes even after returning to the farm?"

"Waste not, want not, you know. Besides," she shrugged, "I always figured I'd use them in a quilt or something someday. But they were really too nice to cut up."

He seemed to be thinking that her keeping the clothes after all this time should be telling her something, but to her relief he didn't voice his thoughts out loud. One by one, they passed through the metal detectors. When they emerged on the other side of it, he said softly, "I always wondered how you'd look in jeans. Now I know." His eyes darkened sexily. "You look great."

That threw her. She had expected him to be disappointed. He wasn't. "Sure you don't like me better in a dress?" she goaded lightly.

He grinned and leaned down to whisper in her ear. "I like you best in nothing at all." He straightened, his blue eyes twinkling merrily. "I just haven't seen you that way in awhile." But he would, his grin seemed to say.

Rebecca concentrated on getting to the right gate. When they had, she got out her ticket. "Is Andy a good traveler?"

"He has been so far." Jack paused. His glance turned serious. "Why did you change clothes?"

Rebecca sighed. "I don't like being stared at, and I have a feeling my Amish dress would earn me plenty of stares in California."

For a moment Jack looked like he wanted to disagree with her about that but the moment passed without comment from him. "While you were in the ladies' room, I talked to my friend, Russ Saunders. Everything's set for your showing at the gallery tomorrow night, but I have to warn you, Rebecca. He's made a big deal about the fact that you're bringing authentic Amish work with you. He's going to expect to see you in Amish clothing.''

Rebecca burned with sudden resentment. She scowled at Jack as they boarded the plane and settled in their seats. ''Then he's going to have to be disappointed because I'm no one's public exhibit, or Amish fantasy.''

But Jack only grinned again. ''You're wrong about that,'' he said, leaning down to whisper in her ear. ''You're my fantasy, Rebecca. And you always will be.''

Silence fell between them. The next few minutes were taken up with getting in their seats. Jack settled Andy into his infant seat, in the seat next to the window, then sat down in the middle seat, so that he was between her and Andy.

As soon as he was settled, he took her hand in his and held it tightly. ''I'm glad you came with me.''

Rebecca looked into his dark blue eyes and saw only sincerity. She regarded him warily. ''Why?''

He smiled gently. ''I want you to see my home out there.''

Rebecca stared past Jack and Andy, out the window, as the big commercial jet backed out of the gate and began the slow taxi toward the runway. ''You think I'll be tempted to stay in California, don't you?''

Jack waggled his eyebrows at her and gave her hand another squeeze. ''A guy can always hope,'' he quipped.

She shook her head and sent her glance heavenward. She knew this was all still a fantasy to him. But life wasn't like a movie. There were no easy answers, and often, no happy endings. Not for people like them. "Jack, you are such a dreamer."

His eyebrows climbed. "And you're not, I suppose."

Rebecca shrugged, aware it wasn't fear she was feeling now so much as excitement to be with him. "I'm not in a league with you," she said lightly, instructing herself to keep her defenses up. Though she sensed that was an activity more easily decided than accomplished.

Jack studied her with detached thoughtfulness. "Then why did you decide to come with me?" His glance narrowed faintly as he waited for her answer.

Because I want to make love to you without fear of interruption, or discovery, Rebecca thought. But she was also afraid that if she did make love with him she would be in over her head...

Hours later, they landed at LAX. Rebecca held Andy while Jack collected their luggage and the boxes of quilts, found a skycap to help him load everything on a cart and went out to long-term parking to pick up his car. Rebecca stood at the curb, Andy in her arms, the warm sunshine swirling around them. If this was a dream, she thought, feeling ridiculously happy and relaxed and free of curious public scrutiny, she didn't want to wake up.

The skycap turned to her with a friendly grin. "You folks glad to be home again?"

Not wanting to get into the story of her life, Rebecca nodded.

"Where you all traveling from?" the skycap continued.

"We flew out of Philadelphia," Rebecca said.

The skycap made a comical face. "Whoa. Cold out there, isn't it?"

"Very," Rebecca said. Although Jack hadn't seemed to mind the weather. Traveling by horse and buggy... now there was another matter.

"Well, you got a cute baby and a pretty nice looking husband," the skycap said as Jack pulled his Mercedes SL Coupe up to the curb. "A very nice car. And great weather here in Los Angeles. What more could you want?"

Indeed, Rebecca thought as Jack popped the trunk, and he and the skycap began the process of loading everything into the car. "You and your husband have a good day now," the skycap said after Jack had tipped him.

Jack got into the car, grinning hugely. "Husband?"

"I didn't want to go into long explanations," Rebecca said, pink-cheeked.

"This is what it would be like, you know," Jack said in a deep, satisfied voice. "The three of us, traveling around. Together. With every luxury imaginable."

Yes, Rebecca thought, but would you love me, Jack? Not just today or tomorrow but forever? That was what she really wanted to know. If she could believe it, then everything would be different. If she could believe it, she just might take the leap, chuck everything familiar once again and marry an Englishman.

Chapter Twelve

"So what do you think?" Jack asked as he shifted a sleeping Andy a little higher in his arms.

Rebecca looked around his trilevel home in the Hollywood Hills. She had expected his home to be luxurious, and it was. She just hadn't expected it to be this cozy or welcoming. Like her grandparents' farmhouse, this place had wood floors that were polished to a golden glow. Area rugs were scattered here and there. There was a massive fireplace with a fieldstone hearth in the family room, a sunny well-equipped kitchen with a dishwasher and a microwave, four bedrooms—three of which were completely empty—and three bathrooms. His study ran the entire length of the house, and had two computers, several printers, a fax machine, copier and...a Nordic track? She turned to him in surprise.

"When I get blocked, a little exercise helps," he said.

Rebecca nodded. Aware he was waiting to hear her reaction, she said, "Your home is beautiful, Jack."

He grinned, pleased. "Ah, but the question is, can you see yourself living here?"

Her throat dry, her pulse racing, she smiled. "You're pushing me, Jack."

He merely raised a brow at her soft-spoken warning. "And you're evading."

She strode nearer, aware her nipples were beading beneath the T-shirt and bra. She told herself it was because she wasn't used to being in air-conditioning. Cupping her hands beneath opposite elbows, she said, "Don't you have to go to the studio?"

"Tomorrow morning." Jack placed a sleeping Andy in his Portacrib, then walked to her side. "Tonight is all ours." He came up behind her, his front to her back, and put his hands lightly on her shoulders. "So what would you like to do?"

Rebecca knew they had to do something or they'd end up in his bed in about two minutes. She turned around to face him. Her heart was racing. Lower still, she tensed in all too familiar anticipation. "I'd like to see one of your movies."

Jack dropped his hands with a frown. "I don't have anything in the theater right now, but I've got them all on videotape—"

Rebecca smiled. "Sounds perfect," she said.

SIX HOURS, three feedings, four diaper changes later, Andy was finally ready to go to bed for the night. Jack put him down while Rebecca finished watching his Western, *Beneath a Blazing Sun.*

It had been a long day, starting with the drive from the farm to the airport, then the flight, then the trip back to his place, the rigamarole of getting settled, ordering dinner in. Jack knew he should be tired. He wasn't.

He felt as if he could go another twenty-four hours. Looking at Rebecca, who showed no signs of drowsiness, he guessed the same was true for her.

Jack switched off the VCR and, pretending not to see the tears running down her face, he took her hand and led her out back to the deck that ran across the entire width of the house. It overlooked both his lagoon-style swimming pool and the heavily populated canyon below. The night stars shone above. Jack was achingly aware that they had less than forty-eight hours left together in California. Then she'd be on a plane back to Pennsylvania. He'd have to decide whether to follow her back or cut his losses and stay here, alone with Andy.

He hadn't changed his mind about wanting her to be a central part of his life. That would always remain the case, he suspected. But he wasn't sure if she would ever allow herself to trust him. And trust was something he couldn't live without.

Jack looked down at Rebecca. She was still choked up, tears running down her face.

He grinned, remembering he'd felt the same aching sadness when he'd written the screenplay. Perhaps the two of them weren't so far apart in their thinking after all, he thought, encouraged by that sign of oneness. Perhaps all Rebecca needed was time to gather

her courage, so that she could go to her grandparents and tell them the truth, and then claim her son, marry him, and move to Los Angeles, permanently.

"Come on, the movie wasn't that sad," he teased, taking her into his arms.

To his delight, Rebecca didn't fight him. She leaned into the solid male warmth of his chest. At that moment, her life in Pennsylvania seemed very far away to Jack.

She gazed up at him, her expression serious, admiring to the point of utter devotion. Jack felt another thrill slide through him. She respected his work. That was one barrier down.

"You're a very talented writer, Jack," she said softly.

He grinned, wondering if there was ever a time she didn't look beautiful, and wiped away a tear with a thumb. "So they keep telling me," he drawled, trying without much success not to let her heartfelt praise go to his head.

"You could never give it all up, could you?" she said.

Jack tensed as he realized this conversation was leading to the question of whether he could live in Pennsylvania indefinitely or not. He already knew, from his conversation with the director and the studio head yesterday, that they expected him to be more readily available during the filming of future screenplays than he had been the last week or so.

Marrying Rebecca and moving to Pennsylvania would ultimately mean living a bicoastal life-style he wasn't really sure would be good for any family. Deciding to keep things simple for the moment, he only shrugged and said, "I'm a writer, Rebecca. I can write anywhere. Even in a loft, if I have to. I thought I'd proved that."

"Yes," she said calmly, still studying his face with relentless scrutiny, "but that was very uncomfortable."

"True." Jack nodded briefly, recalling first the hours in the cold, drafty loft, then the hour or so he'd spent with her, alone up there. At that memory, he couldn't help but grin. "Until you arrived on the scene, anyway," he teased.

"Don't mock me about that."

"Who's kidding?" Jack said earnestly, still holding her against him, length to length. "You fulfilled any number of my fantasies that night."

Rebecca inhaled sharply. Her thighs trembled against his. "You dreamed about kissing a woman in a hayloft?"

Jack threaded his fingers through her hair. "I dreamed about kissing *you* in a hayloft. Now the car..." He couldn't help but grin rapaciously again at the delicious memory. "The car caught me by surprise."

She flushed, embarrassed by the frank, sexual talk, then shook her head in silent, mocking reproof. "You're incorrigible," she said sternly.

"Insatiable," he corrected quietly, bending his head to kiss her softly, sweetly. "I'll never get enough of you, Rebecca. Never."

Their mouths mated again in a tumultuous kiss.

The next thing Rebecca knew she had been swept up into his arms. Jack was carrying her up the stairs to his bedroom. And she knew even before he laid her gently on the bed that she wasn't going to stop him. Not this time. Not the next.

Jack hadn't intended to make love to Rebecca during her stay in Los Angeles. Just kiss her and hold her and remind her how much they had meant to each other, one night, one very special night, long ago. But the moment her lips warmed beneath his and her mouth opened to receive his tongue, the moment her body turned all soft and fluid and giving, he knew he wasn't going to stop with just one kiss or even two. He was going to make love to her, if she let him, and it seemed very much as if she was going to let him. He pushed his knee between hers, parting her legs, then shifted his weight inside the warm cradle of her thighs.

"I want to make love with you again," he whispered as he touched the satiny curve of her waist, the subtle drape of her hip. "I want to kiss you everywhere, touch you everywhere...and in every way," he said, rolling so they were lying side by side on his bed, facing each other. He slid a palm down her thighs, between her knees and felt her quicken restlessly against his touch as her torment and pleasure tangled. "But if I'm going too fast for you, all you have to do is say no," he promised in a low whisper, gently caressing the tender area between her knees, deftly but slowly urging them apart as he unzipped her jeans, "and I'll stop."

But to his pleasure, she didn't say no, not when he touched her intimately, smoothing his palms down her hips, between her thighs, not when he touched and kissed her breasts. Not when he gave in to the urgency driving them both and gave up the pleasure of simply caressing her and slipped inside her. Desperate for more, she reached for him. He held her tightly, one arm anchored firmly around her hips, lifting her slightly. His mind awhirl with the torrent of need flowing through his veins, he deepened his possession of her. She moaned soft and low in her throat and moved restlessly against him, but Jack remained as he was, buried deep inside her. He couldn't take much more, not without losing control. And though he wanted that, he wanted to find a way to pleasure her first, a way that would give her the ultimate release.

"Jack," she said again, stirring against him, writhing in pleasure, shuddering with release as he touched her there. And then she was gripping his hips, moving against him. The fragile thread of his control snapped. The passion that had been suppressed exploded into an eager kiss. She moaned again, willing him on, meeting each demand with one of her own. Until his hips rocked urgently against hers, infusing her with shuddering sensation. And it was only then, when he knew she had experienced the complete wonder of their love anew, when her eyes were cloudy with desire, that he let his own passions govern.

Surrendering to a desperate hunger, he braced his weight with his hands on either side of her, buried himself to the hilt and rocked against her slowly, so slowly, wanting to draw their loving out forever even as he pushed them both toward the edge. Her face lifted to his, she inhaled sharply, and their mouths met in a searing, sensual kiss. Again and again, they drew from each other, pouring out all that was in their hearts and in their souls, pouring out all the things they wanted to say, and still had no words for.

Until that night, Jack hadn't known his control could be so easily lost, but it was. He hadn't known she could want so desperately, but she did. He groaned as their tongues twined urgently and his body took up a primitive rhythm all its own. The bedroom grew hot and close. Their clothes, half on, half off, crushed between them. And yet, mostly he was aware of Rebecca, the welcoming power of her love, the soft, sweet, wild yearning he felt rising inside her.

But it wasn't only Rebecca that was experiencing this wild flood of pleasure. He was feeling it, too, the incredible intimacy of their lovemaking almost as overwhelming as the sheer luxury of having her in his arms again. He was aware of every soft, warm inch of her, inside and out. Every pulsation. Every sigh of desire and whimper of need. Burning with his need for her, savoring the sweetness of her unexpected acquiescence to his body's demands, he shut his eyes, and let himself go where she led. Lost in the maelstrom of pleasure, lost in everything but the sunny, springlike scent that was her and the soft yielding of her body, he went deeper, deeper yet.

Whimpering slightly, she clutched him closer and rose to meet him. Drunk on the power of their love, overcome with need, he plunged higher and found her hips lifting in an effort to take him even higher. His control shattered, he hurtled into the sweet oblivion of release. She went with him, rushing headlong into the storm.

When it was over, he held her close, wishing they could stay that way forever. "This is just the beginning for us, Rebecca," he whispered in a low, tender voice that warmed her from the inside out. "Just the beginning." And as he possessed her again, heart, body and soul, she began to think it was.

FINALLY EXHAUSTED, they lay in each other's arms. Rebecca had never felt so content or so free. This night, this whole week, had been something of a miracle for her. She wasn't used to losing track of her common sense. She wasn't used to giving herself over to reckless heartfelt abandon. But she had done just that with Jack, not just once now, but twice. Was the fact she couldn't seem to stay out of his bed some sort of sign they were meant to be together, as Jack insisted, or was it a sign of her own lack of character?

"I keep telling myself not to get involved with you," she admitted with a sigh. She wasn't sorry they'd made love, yet neither was she one hundred percent at peace about it. If not for the baby, Jack wouldn't have come back to her. And that bothered her more than she wanted to admit.

"That's funny," Jack said softly, "'cause I keep trying to figure out how to get you involved."

Rebecca propped her chin on her hand and studied him. She wanted to believe he was serious about her, not just for now but for all time; she just wasn't sure she could. But maybe it was time she started to find out. "Could you live in Pennsylvania?" she asked finally.

He smiled at her, laced a hand through the hair at the back of her neck and brought his mouth back to hers. "I think the real question is, Rebecca," Jack said as he bent his head to kiss her thoroughly once again, "could you live in Los Angeles?"

JACK'S QUESTION stayed with her long after they made love again, and then fell asleep, and it was still with her the following morning when Jack, Rebecca and Andy arrived at the movie set. The warehouse-like soundstage contained numerous sets. An Amish store, the inside of an Amish home. An Amish school. The three of them stood in the foreground as the actors did a scene. It looked fine to Rebecca but the young, bearded man in the director's chair was far from satisfied.

As soon as the director yelled "Cut!" another man in a bill cap hurried toward them. He had a clipboard in his hand and a worried look on his face. "Jack, glad you're here. We need some work on the dialogue. Listen to the run-through, and see what you can do to make it a little snappier..."

Rebecca stepped back, Andy still in her arms. Aware she was in the way of cameras, crew, makeup people, she roamed farther away from the activity. Andy was sleeping now, curled peacefully against her breast. Holding him close, inhaling his sweet baby scent, she felt a certain serenity, and a temptation to claim him as her own. "If only you were mine," she whispered as Andy began to stir against her. Things would be so much simpler. She would know what to do: marry Jack.

Her hand rubbing Andy's back, she moved farther away from the action, and came upon a set resembling the inside of a barn.

It was different from theirs, of course. Longer, wider, more old-fashioned, with a dirt floor instead of cement, but the hayloft was the same, the ladder leading up to it the same.

Footsteps sounded behind her. Rebecca turned to see a young woman with a clipboard coming toward her. Seeing the sleeping baby, she smiled at Rebecca and whispered, "Jack asked me to check on you."

Rebecca whispered back, "I was afraid Andy was going to wake. I didn't want his crying to interrupt the filming."

"Good thinking. Cute kid. Someone said he was Jack's?" The question hung in the air.

Forcing herself to retain a cheerful expression, Rebecca nodded. "And yours?" the young woman continued.

I only wish, Rebecca thought. She shook her head. The young woman lifted a skeptical brow but said nothing. She turned to the loft. "Nice, isn't it?"

Rebecca nodded. "They filmed the pivotal love scene there, yesterday. You know, the one Jack just rewrote. It was pretty good. Sensual anyway."

Without warning, Rebecca felt as if she could hardly breathe, but somehow she found her voice. "Did he say why he rewrote it?"

The young woman nodded. "Yeah, he said his fantasy had always been to make love in a hayloft. Guess since it had never happened, he wrote it instead."

Don't bet on that, Rebecca thought bitterly, and with great depth of feeling. They hadn't actually made love, of course, but they had talked intimately and kissed each other passionately.

Recalling how she had revealed her innermost feelings to Jack that night, she felt ill inside. Like she'd been used in the most heartless way possible. She'd thought Jack was different, but he was just like Wesley, looking for a pure and innocent girl to make his dreams come true. Someone to help him visualize and at least begin to act out the pivotal love scene he'd been having such trouble writing.

"Jack mentioned you're from Pennsylvania?" the young woman continued.

Again, Rebecca nodded. It was a struggle to retain her smile, but she was determined not to be any more humiliated in public than she already had been by Jack in private. More than ever, she was glad she hadn't worn her Amish clothes.

"He said he had to go back to do research last week," the young woman continued, shaking her head in remonstration as she confided with an indulgent laugh, "but of course we all know he was just having a good time."

At that, it was all Rebecca could do not to hunt Jack down and slay him. "A good time?" She choked out the words.

"Yeah, soaking up the local color. He's always been like that. Did he ever tell you about the year he worked on the updating of *The African Queen?* He got so far into the research all he wanted to do was go on safari-style river trips. Fortunately for all of us, he eventually got it out of his system and moved on to another project. Otherwise we probably never would have gotten another screenplay out of him."

Bitterness welled inside her. Her eyes felt hot and dry. The inside of her chest was one massive ache. "How long did it take?" Rebecca asked calmly, feeling oddly detached, as if she were too numb inside to be truly devastated . . . yet. The numbness would wear off in time.

The young woman shrugged. "I can't really remember. A couple months maybe—"

In the distance, there was a round of laughter from the set. The young woman smiled. "Sounds like they got it right that time." She moved off in the direction of the soundstage where the action was being filmed.

Too bad she and Jack hadn't, Rebecca thought.

"YOU'VE BEEN AWFULLY QUIET. Are you nervous about tonight?" Jack asked as Rebecca met him in the foyer of his Hollywood Hills home.

She was wearing a plain emerald-green dress, another leftover from her married life. She shook her head. "Just anxious to be leaving," she said coolly.

Jack had already said goodbye to the baby-sitter he'd hired and to Andy, so he followed her down the walk to the car. He shoved his hands into the pockets of his trousers, and matched her steps. "I'm sorry it took so long on the set today."

"I'm not," Rebecca said tightly. "I learned a lot."

He narrowed his gaze. "Did someone say something to you?"

The pulse pounded in Rebecca's throat. If she hadn't been so angry with him, she would have appreciated how handsome he looked in the sophisticated navy blue suit, striped shirt and tie. But she was angry with him, and she wasn't going to let herself forget why.

She tilted her chin up at him and stopped walking. "What could anyone have said to me to make me angry with you?"

He lifted his hands in mute speculation and held her level gaze. "I don't know," he said brusquely, his confusion evident. "But everything was fine when we got there. Since we left the studio, you've barely been speaking to me."

Suddenly Rebecca didn't want to get into it. "I told you," she repeated impatiently. "I'm anxious to be leaving."

Jack trapped her between the car door and his body. His shoulders were rigid with tension. "And I think it's more than that."

They regarded each other like two prize fighters about to step into the ring—or two lovers about to kiss and make up in bed. Rebecca suddenly decided it was politic to change the subject. She drew a deep breath and asked calmly, "Who is this woman who's sitting for Andy tonight?"

"The director's mother. Don't worry. Andy will be fine."

Rebecca turned toward the car and waited for him to unlock and open the passenger door for her. "Why would I be worried? He's your baby."

Jack leaned against the car, and gave her a hard look. "You know," he drawled, his dark blue eyes glittering dangerously, "if Russ Saunders hadn't gone to such lengths to show your quilts this evening, I'd pursue this here and now."

"Lucky for me he did, then."

"Don't think it's over, because it's not."

Oh, yes it is, Rebecca thought. As much as I don't want it to be, it is.

The gallery was packed. Russ was as disappointed as Jack had said he would be that Rebecca wasn't in Amish dress. "I thought...well, it would've been good for business," he said, "had you worn one of those hats and—"

"Kapps and aprons," Rebecca supplied wearily. She really did not want to get into all this now. She just wanted to sell her quilts and get out of here.

"Right," Russ said.

She looked into his eyes again and saw only kindness. Guilt swiftly followed. In a gentler, more polite tone, she explained, "While I'm out here in Los Angeles, I'd prefer to just blend in."

Russ frowned. "Isn't that against Amish beliefs?"

"Rebecca's always been at least half English," Jack supplied hastily.

"Oh." Russ smiled at Rebecca as if nothing further needed to be said. He took her arm above the elbow. "Come on, let me introduce you around," he offered amiably. "There are a lot of people here who want to know about the unique designs. Jack tells me you've designed many of the quilts yourself—"

The rest of the evening passed in a blur. Rebecca talked until she was almost hoarse, explaining which quilts were done in traditional Amish patterns, and which were unique.

"Is it true Jack found you on one of his trips east to research that new movie he's working on?" a woman asked as she got out her checkbook and prepared to pay an astronomical sum for a quilt to hang on her wall.

"She's not a souvenir," Jack said. He looked irritated.

"Sorry," the woman said. She stammered and turned pink. "I meant—"

"We know what you meant," Rebecca said smoothly. She turned to Jack, giving him a bright, accusing look only he could see before she finished with all the noncombativeness the general public had come to expect from the Amish. "And I guess in a way, I am a souvenir."

She just didn't want to be one.

Chapter Thirteen

"How long are you going to stay angry at me?" Jack asked as soon as they had walked the sitter out to her car and watched her drive away.

Clamping her hands against her middle, Rebecca turned and started up the pebbled front walk to his door. "Probably forever, but that's okay, since I sold all of the quilts and made quite a profit for the folks back home."

He slipped inside the house, and closed the door behind them. "Careful, you might sound mercenary."

She whirled to face him, the depth and breadth of her anger sending her emotions into high gear. "Better than sounding hopelessly cruel," she shot back.

Irritation flashed in his glance and his jaw turned to iron. He put a hand on her shoulder, turned her around and marched her toward the deep sofa in the living room. "Now that remark you are going to have to explain," he said as he sat down beside her. His dark blue eyes searched hers with laser accuracy. "What's making you so angry?" he asked gently.

Her cheeks burned with humiliation and suddenly she found she couldn't look at him after all. "You used me," she said in a low, shaky voice.

He tucked a finger beneath her chin and guided her face back to his. His expression was perplexed. "How do you figure that?"

Rebecca's heart was racing. Looking into his eyes, she could hardly believe it was true, but all she had to do was remember back to the hayloft set she'd seen at the studio, to realize the way she had been duped. And that realization made her feel sick inside. "Because I heard all about the way you operate," she said in a quavering sigh, her eyes dry but burning with both anger and shame. "I heard about the way you really 'get into your research' while you're writing your movies." Unable to bear his nearness any longer, she propelled herself to her feet. Arms folded and pressed tight against her waist, she paced back and forth. "I heard all about that love scene they filmed in the hayloft set the day before we arrived—"

"Hey." Jack bounded to his feet and cut her off. He arrowed a thumb at his chest. "That love scene was written way before we got together. I *sold* that screenplay based on what happens in that scene."

She believed he *had* imagined being in a loft with an Amish woman long before it had happened. That was what made it all so terrible, the thought that the romantic interlude they'd shared wasn't nearly as spontaneous as she had believed. "And once it was written, sold and filmed you decided to experience a bit of romance yourself, is that it?" She had been such a fool!

"You decided to use your tryst with me to add the finishing touches to the scene you'd already written?"

Jack stiffened uncomfortably, but his gaze never wavered from hers. "Kissing you up there was in many ways like a dream come true for me. But if you're accusing me of bundling with you that night only to work out some problem in the writing of that scene or fulfill some romantic fantasy I had then you're wrong."

"Am I?"

"Yes." His mouth thinned to a tight white line. He strode forward, closing the distance between them in two quick strides. Hands on her shoulders, he held her in front of him. "I kissed you that night because I wanted to be with you," he said softly.

How she wished things were different, Rebecca thought wistfully, even as feelings of torment welled inside her. How she wished they had met at some other time, some other way. But they hadn't, she reminded herself firmly as she struggled with the melting desire that filled her every time she was near him. And like it or not, it was time to take a good, hard look at their love affair, and that's all it was. A love affair. He was willing to marry her, of course, because of Andy, but Andy wasn't even her child.

She pivoted away from him, feeling lost. And hurt. And scared. The only cure she knew for that was to be held in Jack's arms. And that she couldn't allow. So she couldn't stay, she thought simply as she raced up the stairs to the bedroom.

He was fast on her heels, taking the stairs two and three at a time, catching up with her as she raced into the bedroom and grabbed the valise she had packed earlier. "Now where are you going?" he demanded, putting himself between her and the door.

Ignoring him, Rebecca walked over to the phone and picked up the receiver. She stared down at the number she had looked up earlier and written on the pad beside the phone. She had known she had to leave as soon as they returned from the showing. Before they made love again. "I'm going to call a cab," she said flatly. She turned her gaze away from his, struggling hard to keep the hurt and the disappointment she felt out of her gaze.

He stepped closer, every inch of him gentling as he neared her. "Why?" he asked softly.

Without warning, hot angry tears burned her eyes. She blinked them back. "Because it's time for me to go home," she said in a strangled voice.

"Wait a minute," he said. "Your flight doesn't leave until tomorrow."

"Then I'll spend the night at the airport."

He regarded her grimly. She knew in that moment she had just hurt him as deeply and effectively as he had hurt her. "You're that anxious to get away from me?" Jack said. In the distance, Andy woke and began to wail.

Rebecca swallowed and began punching numbers on the phone. "I'm that anxious not to be hurt," she said.

"LOOK, ANDY, it's not as if we didn't try," Jack said in the lonely silence that fell after Rebecca left. He put the empty bottle of formula aside and held Andy upright against his shoulder. "We tried our hardest. But Rebecca just wouldn't listen to us. We have to accept that and go on, alone. We can make it without a mom."

Andy gurgled in response and butted his head against Jack's shoulder. Jack took that for a sign of dissension on his son's part, and lifted Andy a little higher, so they could look at each other man-to-man. "I get the point," Jack said. He lowered his son back to his shoulder and patted Andy gently on the back. "You don't want to be without a mom. But honestly now, what choice did we have but to let her go? I can't keep invading her home in Pennsylvania. And she refuses to stay here one minute longer.

"Hell, she won't even admit that she's your mom. In her heart, sport, I know she loves you every bit as much as I do. And that puzzles the heck out of me. If ever I'd met a woman I thought was honest and blunt-spoken to a fault, it was Rebecca."

Jack frowned.

Andy burped loud enough for them both to grin.

"You don't suppose Rebecca could actually have been telling the truth all along, do you?" Jack put Andy down on his lap again.

"Nah," Jack said. "'Cause if that were the case, why wouldn't she have absolutely insisted I call the police and find your real parents?" Jack sighed. He had no answers for anything. He only knew that he had never felt lonelier or more bereft in his life.

Andy wrapped his fist around the end of Jack's index finger as Jack continued glumly, "I know what you're thinking, kiddo, that there must be something more I can do. But there just isn't. I've done everything I could to prove my love to her. Your mom—for whatever reason—just didn't buy it." Jack heaved a sigh of regret and looked down into big baby blue eyes that suddenly didn't look as much like Rebecca's eyes as he had initially thought.

"I need a woman who believes in me, who trusts me to do the right thing and not hurt her." Jack continued pouring out his troubles to his son softly. He frowned his irritation. "Rebecca doesn't even think I'm smart enough to know the difference between infatuation and love. She thinks what I felt for her is all part of my powerful imagination, my getting caught up in writing the new screenplay."

Andy stared up at Jack, let go of Jack's finger and waved both fists in the air. Looking down into his tiny cherubic face, Jack explained, "It's not as if there's anything else I can do to fix things."

Andy crinkled his brow, as if to disagree.

"We have to let her go," Jack said sadly.

Or did they?

REBECCA STOOD IN LINE at the airline counter. She had changed back into her jeans and sneakers. She wasn't sure why, but she just couldn't bring herself to resume her Amish life again yet. There was much she loved about it, and much, if she were perfectly honest, that she could easily do without. The good parts included the love of her family and friends, the security inherent in knowing that little of their life there would ever change. The bad parts including doing everything the hard way and the boredom that came with knowing that everything was going to be the same day after day after day. Rebecca liked the city. She liked driving a car. She liked the excitement of never knowing what was going to happen next. She just didn't like experiencing it all alone.

If she and Jack had worked things out...

But they hadn't.

She frowned, feeling both disappointed in herself and accepting of the truth. Maybe it was the fact that she'd spent the first ten years of her life in an English home, but there was a part of her, she realized now—the part that was most closely linked with her parents—that would always remain forward-thinking to a fault. And there was another part of her, the scared little orphan in her, that liked clinging to the safety of old ways.

The line at the airline ticket counter inched ahead slowly. Rebecca sighed. Waiting in line was one part of English life she could do without.

The lady behind her looked equally fed up with the standing around. She had curly white hair, pale green eyes and glasses. She was dressed in a magenta running suit that zipped up the front, and comfortable shoes. "Traveling alone?" she asked Rebecca.

Feeling in need of some human comfort, Rebecca nodded.

"So am I. There was a time when I would've had my whole family here with me. Kids, husband, even the family dog. Now there's just me." The other passenger smiled a little sadly, then continued to explain, "My kids are all grown now and my husband died last year."

Rebecca nodded, taking it all in. "What about your dog?" she asked, shifting her valise to her other hand.

The woman behind her picked up her carry-on bag and moved forward. "He went to live with my son."

Rebecca absorbed that. "You're not going to get another?"

The woman waved a work-worn hand. "I'm too old to chase a puppy around. Maybe if I'd gotten one before Harry died, but..." She smiled wanly once again. "Time marches on, whether you want it to or not."

How well Rebecca knew that. Only now time would march on without Jack.

The other passenger glanced down at Rebecca's hand, and quirked a brow. "You're not married." She sounded both sad for her and surprised.

"No, I'm not," Rebecca said, beginning to feel herself get a little prickly again.

"A pretty young thing like you should be," the woman continued.

Rebecca's shoulders stiffened. "I'm waiting for the right man to come along," Rebecca said, shifting her bag to her other hand.

The woman sighed and sent Rebecca an indulgent look. "Now you sound like my daughters," she said.

The line inched forward slowly once again. Rebecca looked ahead and counted. She was now three people back from the counter. Which meant she had another five- to ten-minute wait. She looked back at the other passenger, glad she had someone to pass the time with. Though she would have much preferred it to be Jack and Andy. "Your daughters aren't married, either?" she ascertained.

The woman shook her head. "Not that that is any big surprise," she confided. Her voice dropped to a conspiratorial whisper. "They're always finding fault with the men they date. One little snafu in a relationship, one wrong or crossed signal—" the woman made a slashing gesture across her throat "—and they're out the door like a shot."

For the second time in as many minutes, Rebecca felt her shoulders stiffen again. "Maybe they had reason to leave," Rebecca said, eyes front as they all moved forward once again.

"And maybe, just maybe, if my daughters had just looked hard enough, and long enough, they would have discovered the problem wasn't such a dilly after all. Maybe they would have discovered they had a reason to stay."

Rebecca suffered a flash of guilt. Had she looked long enough? Had she really taken time to consider the consequences? Or had she just run away rashly?

The woman nudged her. "It's your turn at the counter, honey."

"Oh. Thanks." Rebecca picked up her valise and marched ahead. Her mind still awhirl with guilty thoughts and lost possibilities, she handed over her ticket. "Going back to Philadelphia this morning?" the airline agent asked with a welcoming smile.

Rebecca nodded and wished she could feel as happy about returning as she ought to feel. After all, she was going back home to the old-fashioned farm and grandparents she loved. Normally, after any time at all away, it would make her very happy to be going home again. But not this time. It just wasn't going to be the same without Jack. And she knew she would miss Andy, too, even if she never had quite gotten Jack to believe that that adorable baby wasn't hers.

"Did you have a nice stay?" the agent asked as she typed the numbers on the ticket into the computer, confirming Rebecca's presence at the airport and her seat on the plane.

"It was short," Rebecca said cryptically. *Too short.*

The agent smiled. "Couldn't you extend it?"

Rebecca sighed. "I wish it was that simple—"

Maybe if my daughters had just looked hard enough, they would have discovered the problem wasn't such a dilly after all. Maybe they would have discovered they had a reason to stay...

Did she have a reason to stay, Rebecca wondered. Was she cutting her losses too quickly? Giving up before it was time? So Andy wasn't her child. So what? She knew in the deepest recesses of her heart that Jack's wanting her had nothing to do with finding a nanny for the baby. He had fallen for her the moment they'd met on that dark, stormy night almost a year ago. And if the way he made love to her was any indication, he was still head over heels in lust with her. But was that enough to actually sustain a relationship over the long haul?

He hadn't actually said he had loved her until after the baby had appeared in their lives. But he had kissed her from the very beginning as if he did. More to the point, he had chased her halfway across the country, insinuated himself into her home and her heart. Not because he really needed a mother for his infant son—he was handling Andy just fine on his own—but because he wanted her. But what about his fantasies? a little voice inside Rebecca prodded. What happened when the movie was over, his last-minute revisions on his screenplay finished? Would he move on to someone else, someone who was in some way related to his next project, or would he still desire her, the way she still desired him?

More to the point, how would she feel? Rebecca wondered. The answer was simple. She would continue to love Jack no matter what. She would continue to desire him. And if she found out...for certain...that Andy was Jack's son, a son he'd had with another woman in another one-night stand at Alec's place, during that same research stay in Pennsylvania last spring, what then?

Could she forgive him that?

If he told the truth about Andy's parentage, if he admitted he'd made a mistake in either deliberately or erroneously misleading her about the situation, Rebecca knew she was capable of forgiving Jack, of looking beyond their past and even current mistakes to the future.

The agent paused. Accurately reading the indecision on Rebecca's face, but mistaking the reason for it, the agent said, "It's only a twenty-five-dollar charge if you want to change the return, you know. We can do that for you very easily, even at this time."

Rebecca tightened her hand on her valise. Heaven knew she was tempted to throw caution to the wind and give it another try. Attempt to make Jack level with her. But even if that happened... if Jack admitted that the baby was his and not hers, Rebecca didn't know if Jack would be willing to try to sort things out again and start over. Rebecca didn't know if there would be a workable way for the three of them to be together and still protect her grandparents but suddenly she wanted to try. "I think I'll—"

"Hold it right there, Rebecca!" Jack said.

Rebecca turned to find Jack standing behind her, Andy cradled in his arms. "You're not leaving!" Jack said as Andy grinned at Rebecca and waved at her sporadically with both hands.

Joy burst inside Rebecca's heart with the suddenness of a rocket launch. "I'm not," she echoed wryly, amused to find she and Jack were suddenly of one mind after all. Even if he hadn't yet realized it.

"No, you're not," Jack repeated, his firm voice overriding hers. He cupped a possessive hand around her shoulder. "I let you run away from me once. I am not letting you run away from me again. I love you,

Rebecca. Not because you're Amish. Not because the passion we share is unlike anything I've ever felt or even dreamed I could feel. But simply because you're you."

The words she had longed to hear sent tears of relief streaming down her face. And Rebecca knew she had been right to give him a second chance.

"I know I've handled this all wrong, right from the start." Jack hastened to finish his confession. "I hurried you into something you weren't ready for—"

Rebecca wiped her damp cheeks. "It takes two to tango, Jack," she said, taking her half-processed ticket back from the agent and stepping out of the line. He wrapped his arm around her. She picked up her valise and leaned into his embrace. "I hurried, too." Andy leaned toward Rebecca, expecting a kiss. Rebecca touched her lips to his brow, and was rewarded with another toothless smile.

Together, she and Jack moved to the wall opposite the passenger check-in counter and took up a deserted spot. "And what you said about you being my fantasy," Jack continued huskily, still holding both Rebecca and Andy close. "I admit that is true," he said softly, his eyes lovingly roving her face. "You are my fantasy woman, Rebecca. You're everything I ever dreamed about. You're the woman I've been writing about and longing for all these years. And that is not going to change, no matter what screenplay I'm working on at the moment. I'm still going to want you, too."

Rebecca dropped her valise, and mindful of Andy, who was still in Jack's arms, wrapped her arm around his other shoulder and hugged him as best she could, considering he was still holding his son. "Oh, Jack, I love you, too," she whispered fervently. That said, she tipped her face up to his. He lowered his mouth and kissed her with a thoroughness that left her trembling and weak and made all her doubts about him seem inconsequential.

"Next point," he said gruffly, moving back at long last, while Andy watched them both in grinning, wide-eyed wonder. "I want us to have a life together. And to that end, I'll do whatever it takes. I'll move to Pennsylvania, do my writing there. We can even live half Amish if you want. I don't care what I have to do. I just want to be with you."

Rebecca paused. "What about Andy?"

"Is he yours, Rebecca?" Jack asked hopefully, holding Andy all the closer.

Rebecca shook her head sadly. Tears filled her eyes. "I wish he was," she admitted in a thready whisper as her heart leapt to her throat. "You don't know how much."

Jack's face fell. He looked as crushed as she felt while Andy tossed perplexed looks from both Rebecca to Jack, as if wondering what in the world was going on now!

Rebecca looked at Andy's upturned cherubic face, so sweet and angelic, and felt her heart swell with love. Suddenly it didn't matter to Rebecca who Andy's mother was. "You could tell me if he belongs to you and another woman, Jack," Rebecca said gently. Her gaze meshed with his. "It won't make any difference in how I feel about either of you. I mean that from the very bottom of my heart," she whispered, standing on tiptoe to kiss them both.

"I know you do," Jack said thickly, looking as if he might be blinking back tears at any minute, too. "That's what makes dealing with this so hard."

"Dealing with what?"

"The fact Andy isn't my son." Jack tightened his arms possessively around Rebecca and Andy both. He looked down at Andy, who was curled contentedly against Jack's shoulder. "I've grown so fond of our little slugger here that I really wish I were his daddy," Jack said sadly. Jack looked back at Rebecca. "But if he isn't yours he isn't mine, and now that I know that for certain...well, we'll have to do something about that."

Rebecca was filled with relief, now that she knew for certain that Jack had not been with another woman. Suddenly it was Andy's future that was hanging precariously in the balance. "I guess that means Andy really was abandoned," Rebecca murmured, her heart twisting with the pain as she voiced the possibility.

Again, Andy's brows shot up, as if he just knew he was at the heart of this discussion, even if he couldn't understand all the words.

"So we'll adopt him and bring him up together," Jack said. "That is, if it's okay with you."

"It is."

They were all silent a moment. Andy reached for Rebecca's hair and grabbed a thick strand with his fist. Rebecca grinned at him and gently extricated Andy's hand from her hair.

Jack sized up Andy's crankiness. "Juice time," Jack said as he guided Rebecca and Andy over to a quiet corner of a waiting area. He sat down and removed a bottle of apple-pear juice from the diaper bag he had slung over his shoulder. "Try this, slugger."

Once Andy was happily settled in his arms, Jack looked up at Rebecca and smiled. "We'll get out of here, just as soon as he's finished his juice."

Rebecca sat next to Jack and Andy. She rested one hand on Jack's shoulder, the other twined with Andy's tiny fist. "Jack?"

"Hmm?"

"Did you really think that Andy was my baby until just a few minutes ago?" If so, that explained so much about his behavior.

Jack nodded. "It really threw me when you denied being Andy's mom . . . I mean I was so sure . . . I guess I just wanted so much for us to have a reason to be together." Jack sighed. "And yet, I think somewhere deep inside my heart, I half suspected you might really be telling the truth. I kept trying to tell myself he looked like you, that our being from two radically different life-styles was reason enough for such an adorable little baby being abandoned on Alec's doorstep, but I think I always knew that you had too much love in your heart to ever have deserted our child. Not that way. Not on a stranger's doorstep, even if Alec was home."

"You're right," Rebecca said softly, glad they were finally in accord on this much. She looked up at him tenderly. "I wouldn't have done that. But if you sensed Andy wasn't mine... then why did you stay in Pennsylvania, why did you bring me back here to Los Angeles?" Had it been just to make love to her, to convince her to move out here and be with him again? Was a love affair still all he was offering her?

Jack's eyes darkened. "I stayed because I half believed that he was your child. I wanted to give you the time you needed to sort out your feelings. And I also couldn't bring myself to leave you, not if there was even the slightest chance that the two of us might end up together." Although his arms were full of Andy, Jack leaned over to press a kiss in her hair. "I want you to marry me, Rebecca, just as soon as we can get everything arranged."

Rebecca gulped around the sudden lump in her throat. For the second time in the space of five minutes she found herself crying. She'd never been so absurdly happy in her life. "Yes, I'll marry you," Rebecca said. They sealed their engagement with a kiss, then slowly drew apart. And as Rebecca looked into Jack's eyes, the rest of her doubts slowly faded away. They could make this work. She knew they could.

"The road ahead of us will be tough—" Jack warned.

"My grandparents will understand," Rebecca countered softly. "They know and love you already. And they'll also understand when I tell them I am moving out here to live with you, that it's time for me to resume the life I would've had had my parents never been taken from me when they were."

"You're sure?" Jack paused, a look of concern on his face. "It's a lot to give up."

"We'll still visit. And I can still design quilts, and help support the family in that way. But it's time for me to move on, Jack. To make a life of my own. The kind I want."

"You name it," Jack whispered, leaning forward to kiss her again, "and it's yours."

He kissed her again, and would have gone on kissing her if Andy hadn't let go of his bottle of apple-pear juice and reached up and twined his tiny fist around Rebecca's hair. Rebecca winced as he tugged it. She carefully extricated her mouth from Jack's, and Andy's tiny fingers from her glorious blond locks. "Looks like someone wants out attention," she quipped, amused.

Jack grinned back at her, and then at Andy. An affection-filled moment passed. Finally Jack sighed, "Which brings us to the next question."

"I know," Rebecca said. She cast Jack a worried glance. "What are we going to do about finding Andy's real parents? Where should we start?"

"I've got a friend, Grady Noland, on the Philadelphia police force. He'll tell us how to start the search."

As soon as they got back to Jack's place, Jack dialed Philadelphia. It took several minutes, but finally Jack got Grady on the line. While Rebecca paced back and forth with Andy in her arms, Jack briefly explained their dilemma to his old college pal. "Anyway, Grady, I was thinking we could start our search by talking to someone in Missing Persons, seeing if any babies have been reported missing in the Philadelphia area."

"That won't be necessary," Grady replied abruptly.

"It won't?" Jack blinked in confusion and shot Rebecca a stunned look.

"I know whose baby this is," Grady said.

* * *

Find out whose baby this is by reading *Too Many Mums*, the final book in Cathy Gillen Thacker's TOO MANY DADS trilogy, available in August from Silhouette Special Edition!

SPECIAL EDITION™

COMING NEXT MONTH

SISTERS Penny Richards

That Special Woman!

Tormented by memories, compelled by desire, Cash Benedict was back. And it meant confronting the woman he'd always wanted. Skye Herder had never forgotten Cash, and now she was about to reveal that she wasn't the only person he'd left behind all those years ago…

TOO MANY MUMS Cathy Gillen Thacker

Too Many Dads

Maverick cop Grady Nolan was thrilled to be a dad…until *two* women claimed to be the mother of his child! Grady hoped it was his ex-wife who was lying and that sultry Jenna Sullivan was telling the truth. Would this detective dad solve the parental puzzle?

THE REFORMER Diana Whitney

The Blackthorn Brotherhood

Beautiful Letitia Cervantes was the kind of woman Larkin McKay had been waiting for all his life. So when her eleven-year-old son's rebellious spirit called out to the father in him, would Larkin forget his troubles and bring them together into a family?

FOR LOVE OF HER CHILD Tracy Sinclair

Erica Barclay's goal was to keep her son safe from the people who threatened their small family. When she fell for Michael Smith, she was torn between passion and her love for her child. Could she still protect her son *and* listen to the needs of her own heart?

BUCHANAN'S BABY Pamela Toth

The Buchanans

Rough-and-ready Donovan Buchanan had left a trail of broken hearts along the road to success…and he'd left perky waitress Bobbie McBride with just a little bit more. Sweet little Rose was now four years old—and about to meet the daddy who didn't know she existed…

PLAYING DADDY Lorraine Carroll

Cable McRay was a mystery to Sara Nelson. Every time he looked at her son, she saw the tenderness beneath his stony façade. And every time she looked into his eyes, she saw the passion he tried to resist. But what kept him from the family—and the future—she knew he dreamed of?

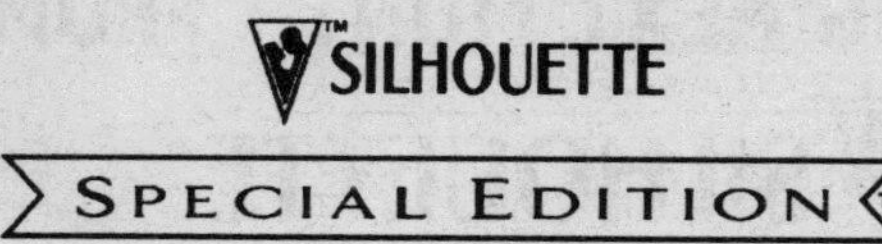

COMING NEXT MONTH

FOR LOVE OF HER CHILD
Tracy Sinclair

ca Barclay's goal was to keep her son safe from the people o threatened their small family. When she fell for Michael ith, she was torn between passion and her love for her ld. Could she still protect her son *and* listen to the needs of own heart?

BUCHANAN'S BABY
Pamela Toth

Buchanans

ıgh-and-ready Donovan Buchanan had left a trail of ken hearts along the road to success...and he'd left perky tress Bobbie McBride with just a little bit more. Sweet e Rose was now four years old—and about to meet the dy who didn't know she existed...

PLAYING DADDY
Lorraine Carroll

ıle McRay was a mystery to Sara Nelson. Every time he ked at her son, she saw the tenderness beneath his stony ade. And every time she looked into his eyes, she saw the sion he tried to resist. But what kept him from the ily—and the future—she knew he dreamed of?

How to enter...

There are ten missing words in our grid overleaf. Each of the missing words must connect up with the words on either side to make a new word—e.g. PAPER-BACK-WARDS. As you find each one, write it in the space provided, we've done the first one for you!

When you have found all the words, don't forget to fill in your name and address in the space provided below and pop this page into an envelope (you don't even need a stamp) and post it today. Hurry—competition ends 31st January 1997.

Silhouette® One to Another
FREEPOST
Croydon
Surrey
CR9 3WZ

Are you a Reader Service Subscriber? Yes ❑ No ❑

Ms/Mrs/Miss/Mr ______________________________

Address ______________________________

____

______________ Postcode ______________

One application per household.

You may be mailed with other offers from other reputable companies as a result of this application. If you would prefer not to receive such offers, please tick box. ❑

C296
A